ACCLAIM FOR WISHES

"Charming and inventive, *Wishes* offers a romance that tiptoes between reality and fairytale. A smart, heartfelt retelling perfect for fans of Kiera Cass and Melanie Dickerson!" – CAROLINE GEORGE, author of *Dearest Josephine*

"Fans of Nadine Brandes, CJ Redwine and Sara Ella need look no further than Brittany Eden for their next ultimately poetic and utterly immersive read. True magic! Eden writes with one of the most naturally talented voices I have read in years!" – RACHEL MCMILLAN, author of *The Mozart Code* and *The Castle Keepers*

"Enchanting and unique, Eden's prose in Wishes is a paintbrush, creating a masterpiece depictiı̇ grief and sorrow and how love can overcome them in time. B beloved fairytales—*Cinderella* and *P.*

beautiful novella that will capture the hearts of readers, young and old." – V. ROMAS BURTON, author of the Heartmaker Trilogy

WISHES

Writing By Brittany Eden

The Heartbooks Series
Wishes
Hearts (forthcoming in June 2023)

The Circus Diary

Poetry in Anthologies
Fool's Honor
The Heights We'll Fly To
The Never Tales: Volume One
Masquerade Anthology (forthcoming)
The Never Tales: Volume Two (forthcoming in 2023)

Short Stories in Anthologies
Candles in the Dark in *Fantasea*
Seasons in a Four Seasons Anthology (forthcoming in December 2022)

WISHES

BRITTANY EDEN

Quill & Flame
PUBLISHING HOUSE

To all the writers shining light through ink spots on ivory pages, and to my mom, dad, and brother—this book was a family affair!

LOIREWALL
GRAY FOREST
COTTAGE
WHITE FOREST
UPPER TOWNE
GARDENS
PALACE
YORKSON TRAGEDY MEMORIAL
TO GABREVILLE
VALAIS BOULVARD
AZALEA'S TREASURES
UNIVERSITY
WIREALEY SQUARE
RUSSET BRIDGE
LOWER TOWNE
N
W
E
S

WISHES

Forty years before
the events in
Hearts...

Chiming bells on holy days ring
Wishes for lost souls sing
Sacred spells, yearning hearts
Loss and love amid the sound
Chiming bells, 'til peace reigns

—"Passing Grief" a lament published anonymously
in *The Loirehall Times*, now the epitaph at the
Yorkson Tragedy memorial

The late King of Loirehall, His Majesty Phillipe
Leopold Irwin II Garcon, Duke of Carlingsen,
and Lady Garcon, late Queen of Loirehall, Duchess
of Carlingsen (from file).

THE LOIREHALL TIMES

DECEMBER 19TH

ROYAL FAMILY PREPARE FOR FINAL MEMORIAL

Article by Rose Connelly, photo by Declan Hayes

THE FINAL TOLL WILL RING JUST PAST 8 O'CLOCK
THE MORNING OF THIS ARTICLE'S PRINTING. THE
CROWN PRINCE WILL PERFORM THE FINAL HONOR
OF RELEASING THE ASHES OF THE LATE KING AND
LADY GARCON, HIS FATHER AND MOTHER.

*Photo: The Regent, his nephews, the Royal Court, and Loirehall's
townspeople line Valais River last year (file photo)*

In an unexpected turn of events, the palace released a statement that Prince Nicholas Garcon would be stepping in for his uncle's last public act as monarch, ending the formal period of mourning. By passing on this last official act to his eldest nephew, observers are calling Duke Erick's decision both heartfelt and worrisome amid rumors of the well-loved regents' declining health and the uncertainty surrounding the House of Garcon as Loirehall completes the transition to a constitutional monarchy. With neighboring Gabreville having already ceded from their royal roots with independence granted ten years ago from the federal government, the young Crown Prince will face governance challenges from within the Kingdom and farther afield from neighboring nations.

After the customary decade and a half long period of mourning, will this symbolic ending set the tone for the future of the Royal Family? As Loirehall's great and small have lined the Valais every year to honor the memories of those lost in the Yorkson tragedy, will politics overshadow the upcoming coronation this winter solstice?

Editor's note: The day before printing, Château Fleur gave no further comment to the questions raised by this columnist, except to say the forecast didn't look fair and remind citizens to bring umbrellas in case of inclement weather.

THE ABSENT ASHES

December 19th, just after 8 o'clock in the morning

A parade of black umbrellas marshal by the riverside. Shields for the storm.

I slip into the back of the crowd; mournful music has already begun.

For the first time in fifteen years of memorials, it's raining, but this prince would never neglect his duty. After long minutes in the downpour, his dark hair is slicked straight against his temple, above his ear, and down the back of his painfully straight neck. From across the Valais River, I cannot see details of his expression or depth in his eyes, though his countenance is formal and unmoved. Still, I know he must feel the chill of the drops of the same morning rain pelting my cheeks. His form is bracketed by unkind winds, but he seems sturdier than I. Steadfast to my sorrow.

The prince who's never seen me is all I've come to see.

I question how certain seconds in life tick longer in time—take longer time—and if the rainfall on his uncovered face hides any tears.

Because of this sopping hour and pouring rain, it would be the only year he could cry, and part of me wishes he could.

No one's private grief should be this public and austere. He is the reason I come every year and spill sorrow. My tears fall as much for my late mother and father as for this young man who can never cry.

I weep for him.

The black satin tied around his arm is wider than it had been fifteen years ago. He'd been a boy three years older than I, all awkward limbs, and the memory of his small, tearless face cannot be swept from mine. Because he lives with pressures and expectations placed upon him in these public moments, I wildly believe my own tears mingle with his unshed ones.

There have been times I've tried to wash it all away, to forget the mourning. Yet we remain in it. Haunted by visions both solemn and wild, I wish to forget the silence of a moment but instead remain, drowning in years of grief, the prince and I pained people only passing on the day we mourn the same loss.

Our parents, gone, quick as a flood. And grief, endless and remembered like the river—surging, surprising. Deadly to that car and those in it caught in the floodwaters.

So, here we are again, on the anniversary of their deaths—the King with his queen and her lady-in-waiting, my mother. Fifteen years ago—only months after the Yorkson Tragedy that I remember only in vague, random pictures, as I was too small—my father had soon followed them into the next plane of otherworld. His death is still a lost mystery to me.

Now, we are waiting for the final sprinkling of ashes into the rising river that took them, on this, the last memorial since crowds first watched. The young prince has become so regal, a perfect Crown Prince, filling into his form and duties. And every year after the funeral and the first memorial, he wore the mourning armband like me, the sheer fabric barely holding brokenhearted children together in loss and silence.

But in this moment, though I'm eighteen and taller than my friends, I still feel like the little girl crying in the crowds, unable to see beyond the adults blocking her view.

Now, I'm watching from behind gathered townspeople. The somber assembly spills five rows deep from the river. Escaping the nearby alley, an orange tabby is chased by rowdy boys, so I hold out the edge of my cloak for it to hide beneath. Puddles between broken cobblestones swallow the small paws beside my cold feet. At least I have boots.

I don't want to look, but like the rest of the crowd, my eyes are drawn across the river. The far side of the water a world away.

Beside the prince is his trusted friend, but though the stylish young man stands at his friend's shoulder, he could never carry this weight. Nearby, the young Captain and an honor guard stand at attention, their respectful distance somehow still intrusive.

The royal court and trusted aides cluster behind the Crown Prince's younger brother, who stays in the background. Only four years separate him from his older brother, but he's not yet strong enough to share the burden of responsibility left by an aging and weakened regent, the Duke, their limping great-uncle who will soon pass on the Crown—the royals in the throes of transition. The House of Garcon, the desolate family.

Leaving his rain-shield with the matronly Azalea—a member of the royal court, of no relation to the royals, who's just lost her own umbrella to the tangle of sweeping winds—the prince steps out alone.

With wooden steps to the edge, he empties the ashes into the river. After all these years, every last speck of dead dust is at last used up. It pains me how far they made those dead ashes go for this memorial, and it pains me that the customary mourning for the royal family had to continue until the year of the next coronation—this year. This blessed year.

Fifteen years has been too long.

The Valais surges toward the far-off lake, drinking up the last traces of the dust, the river's wintertide pace a cruel reminder of all we'd lost in the canal rising and dikes breaking—a terrible day, the Yorkson Tragedy. Now, all that remains of the past is floating down the swelling river.

The prince replaces the jar in his breast pocket, near his heart, absent ashes.

Surrounded by others but always a step ahead, he is fully alone. Like I am alone, always an unnoticed step behind the crowd.

A moment of silence reigns. Heavy hearts punctuated by heavy rainfall. Countless umbrellas cast dark shade and echo falling rain. The weight is unbearable.

As his dark head rises to acknowledge the people gathered, I swear the prince's gaze grazes mine, and I involuntarily step back. It would be the first time our parallel paths had crossed the unsurmountable distance. We are connected, but we have never collided.

There is no rest in his eyes. I take in his rain-darkened hair and beneath a long jacket, his fitted dress suit trimmed with teardrop stars on gold lapels.

Royal grieving thankfully ending, I wish to tell him it was unfair. That his childhood was framed by the yearly remembrance of private pain. That his countenance was beautiful in sorrow. That these bookends on our time of mourning, bookends from the ending of our childhood to the beginning of adulthood, are black and not gold. Empty of color and without a sparkle of hope.

But more than that, I wish to tell him his story isn't over. He's been gone abroad for five years, returning every year for this memorial, but only staying a day. Now, he's back, and he'll stay for good.

For he must become King.

I take another step away. Being at the back of the crowd, it's easy to slip away. Every other eye is riveted to the black-haired Garcon men—the Crown Prince returned for good.

There's royalty, and there's family. He is the essence of both losses. Every year the unanswered questions. We can't control life's rains, but the unfinished story remains. The *why*.

I think of my mother, who drowned with his parents that fateful day. Why did someone so lovely die so suddenly? Why do mothers not live to stroke the hair of growing children?

I think of his mother and father, the monarchs. Why did their car veer into the flooding waters? Why were they there at all, and why didn't they simply drive the other way? Would they have been happy the two young princes weren't with them when they died?

The prince's loss, so like our own, made that day of the tragedy a memorial for many. A day to remember, to honor, to heal.

For this we loved him. For this, I despised him.

December 19ᵗʰ, just a few steps later

I hide. Well, I run first. Down empty cobblestoned alleys, past the ever-lit lamps glowing from the opaque square windows on the brick-fronted entrance to my publisher, *The Loirehall Times*. I refuse to think about the article I wrote for today, and about the new story my boss—publisher Augustus Finley—has asked me to investigate.

I run away from it all. Past the cobbler and candle maker, under clouds so low even the far-off mill leaves its sooty scent on lingering mist. Slipping—then slowing my speed as the bold blue awning of the bookshop comes into view. Ignoring the Gothic spires of Château Fleur in the distance, I duck beneath the corner of *Azalea's Treasures*.

Collapsing onto a patch of dry ground, I rest snug against the window. I mutely chastise the steady downpour, which is strong enough to spatter wetness onto my soaking feet, railing silently at it for already having soaked me and not giving up. I hug my knees to my chest. The lonely streets are a haven for at least another few minutes—the formal processional will take time to disperse the crowd.

With shaking fingers, I unravel my mourning band and close my fist around the soft, wet strip of fabric.

It was my father's necktie. No one wears paisley much anymore, but it's subtle, the velvet design on monochromatic black on black.

I shiver, surprised as the winter-hinting wind awakens the chimes on the ceiling in the path of the door when it opens outward.

The door isn't opening. I'm alone and shuddering. Tingling chimes, dropping drips.

But the drips aren't just the pounding rain. There's a lighter chorus coming from the edges of my cloak, which holds its shape while sopping, dangling against the ground. The navy wool kept at least the journal, my papers, and my notebook with notes about Finley's new assignment in my inner pocket dry. I'll wait for Azalea to return from the ceremony and give her my latest work. I hope she likes it. She is my editor after all, and an important woman in this world. Finley, my publisher, is powerful, but in a seedier way I've never quite trusted. I wish I cared less, and I wish his opinion mattered even less than that.

I sniff. At least I'm writing it.

Scents of rain and pavement steal sorrow from my senses. It's hard to be sad now that I'm alone and there's no one to see my tears. I wipe my face with cold fingers. The past five years of the Crown Prince's absence was a balm and an ache. His yearly return for the memorial was overshadowed by his otherwise constant absence during his obligatory service in an allied neighbor nation's military. I felt it in the depths of the forest where I live. I felt it in the screaming silence of my soul.

My lungs fill themselves with petrichor and I rest my cheek on my knees. My boots are soaked but reliable, worn black leather with a half-inch heel. Shutting my eyes to avoid seeing the scuffs, I wish for another moment to dwell on the face I keep following.

Inside the inner pocket of my cloak, I stroke the golden ribbon and the journal, a gift I never expected to get today.

Flags flap loudly at half-mast, beaten and waterlogged. I don't need to open my eyes to know I can't see the bright gold of the teardrop star waving in the wind, for it's weighed down by black, soaked fabric. I may despise this day more than the rest of the calendar year, but the light feeling of finally letting go of those tears leaves me feeling refreshed, if a bit empty, and maybe a little waterlogged.

Seconds pass quiet and steady. *Tick, tock. Tick*—this is why I love time, when I can steal it for myself. Alone. Away from my step-aunt's vicious voice in the home where she's obliterated any echo of my father's memory and though she stayed with me as my guardian, she's never filled the place in my heart for my lost mother, the step-sister she despised. Lost, a star in a sea of space. I count black droplets on the ground, see rain-soaked dress shoes—

The voice is more marvelous than I could ever have imagined. "Once in a lifetime, headlines read like heralds cry."

A firm hand lands on my shoulder as I scream.

"The world will hear you." The marvelous voice is wry.

"I'm sorry, you startled me." I try to inhale but my throat catches as I look up into mesmerizing eyes. "They're green," I whisper reverently.

Prince Charming's hair flicks over his eyes as he checks over his shoulder. "What's green?"

I shake my head, myself, my shoulder in his grasp. The prince's grasp. *Nicholas.* The voice, the eyes I'd never hoped nor dared to see this close. Close enough to touch and breathing the same air.

"Oh, I can't breathe," I mutter, hands over my pulsing heart.

His hand steadies me until he lets me loose, surprised he's helped me at all. He straightens to his full height beneath the angled corner almost keeping us dry.

"I'm sorry I startled you," he says stiffly, brushing rainwater off his brow, chest rising and falling quickly. Straight eyebrows and perfectly angled sideburns, but his styled hair is flattened by the downpour he clearly just ran through.

I stand, leaning back against cold glass. "Are you really?" I ask. He took my breath away and he's *sorry*? Isn't it his right to interrupt his subject? A Crown Prince should never be sorry. Or should a prince like him always be sorry? I tilt my head, my shock warring with an entirely inappropriate smirk at his unkempt appearance. The attractive upturn of his collar against his hair. "Aren't you supposed to be somewhere?"

He looks down on me with solemn eyes, but a spark of amusement lights their fern-green depths. He's the forest, the moss that never leaves. I want to run into him and never come out.

I don't realize we're leaning towards each other until he pulls back.

"I'm not sure yet." He speaks on an exhale. I can't tell if he's about to laugh or leave. Or if he's shaken too.

Is his heart also racing?

I rush to straighten myself. No slouching. I'm not short, but he's *tall.*

Ding, dong—

We both flinch at the first of the mourning bells and look to the bell tower. How long have I waited for these last tones, the final chimes of my personal mourning bells? I expected peace when it ended, but we're not there yet, as the sound echoes faintly down cobblestoned streets, into misty air. Not quite finished.

The air shifts.

I turn back to find Nicholas kneeling before me, picking up a midnight blue, leather-bound book. Gold silk ribbon page holder. It seems small in his hands, my most valuable possession.

The bells must have soothed the sound of its falling.

He doesn't move with it in his grasp. "What is this?" His voice is so tight, it's almost not a question.

I'm not sure how to answer that my world is so gray that this navy, nearly-black, midnight-blue journal is the brightest color in my life. Or how my world was upended when it was given to me just this morning.

"My father's journal." I speak to his hair, his dark head bent over the palm-sized book of poetry. Flipping pages. Landing long on the last. I breathe in discomfort and a confusing sense of sympathy, which I'd never expected to feel in his presence. A presence which has turned to stone—like a kneeling statue before me. But I can't let this go. "It's mine," I whisper, "please return it, I haven't even—" *read it all yet.* I finish silently.

I only wrote my ending to Father's poem before that appointment in the alley earlier. Now, I extend a hand, and, in another fairylike lifetime, the prince should have reached to place a ring on my finger.

In this life he confounds me.

His gaze trails up my soaked cloak, tracing the muted fire of my fiendish curls, resting on my freckled cheekbones. I imagine my ice-blue eyes are a frozen sky, whereas his are colored like that which thrives in shadows on the forest floor.

He's holding my gaze as if he'd never let me go.

"I finally found you," he says. Pages close with reverence, and he holds the journal loosely.

Questions buzz through my brain: how did he leave the ceremony unnoticed? Did he respectfully bow out for privacy's sake during the final prayers? If he did, why—after all these years of not acknowledging me—has he come here to find me?

But it's almost painful, seeing the pity in the prince's eyes now that he's realized I'm the daughter of the deranged man who died soon after his wife did in the Yorkson Tragedy.

"Give it to me," I say, grabbing his wrist. He flicks me off like a gnat, a startling speed that almost hurts.

It definitely hurts my heart.

One smooth motion and he towers above me again. "No one—" he fists his free hand. "Don't touch me."

I grab the journal, not letting go of it though he pulls at it with long, lean fingers. But I am no buzzing, flying thing to be ignored.

"You," I spit the word, "just touched my shoulder moments ago—"

"Yes. I touched *you*, not the other way around." He clears his throat, muscles working in his neck.

I don't let him continue, tamping down politeness. "Shall I faint and pull the journal on the way down?" I ask. Impertinence be shamed for questioning a broken-hearted girl. "Would you not save me?" I raise a brow, testy, but as unconcerned and aloof as he is, I don't attempt it.

He allows the standoff. It's quiet, the alley still bereft of people. Not that anyone would have willingly ventured out on a day like today.

Strained silence is his answer. Pounding rhythms of rain bookend his stare.

There's a blue tinge in the air. I glance at the cheerfully dripping awning sheltering us from the storm, wincing as wind blows chill rain on my legs.

I try again. "Would you tear it apart? Page by page?" There's a desperate edge to my voice I've never let loose until now. This journal is the truest part of my father I have left, and I've only just discovered it. I feel unmasked. "You have no idea how much this means to me." *You don't know me.* However, he knows my place in the story, so he should understand my rising anxiety.

Unaffected by the rain and the force of my emotion, he all but ignores my tirade. "You startled before because you were avoiding the ceremony," he says.

I gape, altogether impolite now. Fifteen years bearing witness and mourning in silence for *us*—there was never a tear that fell from my eyes that wasn't connected to him and the story running a river between us—and he assumes I hid from this final day, having no courage at all. We both lost our parents that fateful year, but with what I read in my father's newly discovered journal this morning, Nicholas Garcon and I have yet another layer of fate tying our stories together.

"I've never missed a single moment of a single year of the memorial. I'm not, I wasn't—" I'm losing my calm. "How dare you!" Exasperated, I release my hold on the journal.

His drenched jacket pulls against broad shoulders as his hands automatically bind behind his back. The black mourning band tightens around the pleasing shape of his arm. Every limb, from those squared shoulders and that haughty tilt of his neck to the length of his legs appears self-assured. In person, I'd expected manners to be part of his charm, but right now, discipline is engraved along the taught lines of his body; his unshifting stance sure as he assesses my rising desperation.

I just want him to give me back the journal.

"Where do you live?" he asks out of the blue.

I blink. Stars, I could never tell him of my absurd, cruel, nearly bankrupt step-family. Or that Finley's just assigned me a story that might stain doubt on the legitimacy of his role as heir.

The Crown Prince—this infuriatingly stoic young man on the outside with storms behind his eyes—ignores my silence and continues in a smooth, certain voice. "It doesn't matter. I finally found you," he repeats the thrilling, troubling words.

I might swoon, for a dashing young prince like him to know me. At the thought that he'd been looking for me all these years, for the poor soul united with his since that tragic day.

Instead, I stumble back, and my knees knock against the mailbox, rattling the glass bookshop window. His free hand reaches to catch me but stops short. He wears a luxury watch. Thick, black leather band, black face, three bronze hands. Good taste, and I relax slightly at the sight of roman numerals. His choice of timepiece ticks my trust up a notch. Four seconds pass until I let my eyes leave the watch face and look up.

"You know who I am?" I ask belligerently, standing hopefully primly while steadying my shakiness. I flick my gaze at the journal, which he blatantly enjoys ignoring. I can't ignore the questions chasing each other. *He won't take it, will he?*

He almost smirks. "You know who *I* am." It isn't a question.

I snort.

How could anyone in Loirehall not know the Crown Prince? Much less an aspiring newspaper columnist, like me. *He doesn't know I'm Rose Connelly from the paper, does he?*

But his charm is too pointed for me to fully believe him, as his statement seems closer to a question. Either he can't speak punctuation, or he's hiding something.

I stare up at his handsome face. So many years, knowing all we had in common, wondering what it would be like if *he* knew who *I* was—the loss we share. It seems like he might know that I'm that girl, the poor orphan daughter people talked about behind their hands every memorial and the days each year in between. People knowing me usually made them look at me less. What if I never see his face again, now that's he's finally looking at me with that knowledge?

I brace myself for disappointment but hide the churning inside, inclining my head to him. "Charmed to make your acquaintance, prince with no umbrella." I extend my hand expectantly again, wiggling my fingers for the journal.

A short laugh from deep in his chest surprises us both. It sounds perfect, yet out of place. A star too early in twilight. "And why haven't you got one?" Eyes alive, eyebrows raised.

I avoid his seeking gaze and stare at my empty, upturned hand and the memory of earlier this morning.

After I'd walked across town happily secluded from the worst of the rain under my wooden-handled umbrella, I'd encountered my step-aunt, Madame Vera Eugenie Beaumont. She'd forgotten her umbrella this morning and when their car arrived at the riverside and I had what she needed, my step-aunt would never deign any less than me giving some sort of sacrifice. Preferably one that left me uncomfortable and embarrassed. So, she took my umbrella and left me to stand alone and soaked on the road. Far be it from my overbearing step-aunt to consider my welfare or the rain, for I am a straggler, a nuisance. An oddity, to be ignored until what I had could be of use.

Suddenly, his hand hovers above mine, long fingers and sinews. Pulls away. Drawing my eyes to his as he shifts himself slightly nearer and places the journal gently in my waiting hand.

For a second that feels like betrayal, I wish what he placed in my palm was his hand and not Father's journal.

"For losing an umbrella today, I see I'm in good company," he says, and his words flow around his tongue pleasingly, as if he understands. Perhaps the pressures we face are more similar than I imagined. A layer of acceptance covers the emptiness in my heart. He blinks. "What better day for broken souls to meet—" he cuts off the famous line from the motto on his family's crest as our gazes ignite.

It feels like he knows we'd both been returning to the river that took our parents, for all these dark years, while surviving our parallel and entirely separate lives.

Because I don't sleep well, I awaken before the sun. And so, over the years, I'd often looked out the window and felt lonely. Except those days I glimpsed the prince.

I'd seen him rowing on the Valais, before his years abroad. Conquering the river before dawn, always alone. Breaking smooth water with strong strokes. Faster, and as time wore on, he would race by in a sheen of sweat, his face set. He became strong, now the lithe and steady man before me. But then, he was running from something, or pushing toward something. I could never tell the difference, and I figured I'd have to remember how to catch my own breath first—the breath now caught up in his very presence.

We're alone, it feels like the town is empty or time stands still. There is no one now to see him standing before me. Staring. Seeking. *Had he seen me all those years?* His unrelenting gaze rakes over my face, my form. What can he see? All I see is how he's changed from lanky teenaged boy to a young man with a commanding air. The prince who would be King. The boy I pictured as wooden and emotionless so very alive in front of me.

Moss colored eyes narrow, unwavering. "Where do you live?" he repeats the question.

If I speak, it will confirm his question. If I don't, it may not matter. My silence tells its own story—how I've cursed him and wished for him for fifteen long years. How I watched him fight the memories of the river in the wild, northernmost side of Loirehall's Gray Forest. From our cottage, one of the many dotting the sides of the weaving canal scattered past town boundaries, I'd often ventured closer to the path through dense pine trees. Always afraid to be nearer to the water. But for finding him, a glimpse of him, I was sometimes secretly brave. Over the years, he was the courage in my fear and my morning walks became a cinder. Neither of us were flames, our growing-up souls too wounded for anything more than pressing forward. But even that we had to start before others saw us, the first victories of the day too daunting to conquer with an audience.

Does he recognize me? From those days staring from afar in the forest? From the funeral fifteen years ago and every memorial since?

He assesses me. "You live somewhere near the town-line on the north curve of the canal, do you not?" Formal words, edged with desperate certainty. And a lifetime between us as he pauses. "I saw you walking this morning—" but his voice catches. I inhale and hold it in. *He knows I'm the daughter of the lady-in-waiting and he knows I've been hovering like a forest fairy all these years.* I exhale as he leans forward, just an inch. "But who are your family?"

I shake my head. I don't want to share my home or my memories. This connection should've remained a secret I kept for myself, alone. Not for him or anyone else. Because watching the Crown Prince from afar grow into the person he is meant to be has been giving me courage enough to be the person I should be.

I'm trying, but today is proving particularly challenging.

Still, I don't want his pity, just because he's found out my mother died with his parents, and my father soon after that. I'm *that* little girl. The whole town knows *her*; it's why I have a pen name.

I press my eyelids shut but give up on ignoring anything anymore.

"What do you mean, you finally found me?" I finally ask, opening my eyes to examine the dark hair flattened across his forehead. It makes him seem younger, unpolished with that untamed passion filling the disappearing space between us. "Tell me," I say, stronger now.

"Or what?" Restraint is evident in his eyes. *What don't I understand?*

"I'll behead you. Or some such just punishment," I say with a head toss. A flicker of amusement at my outrageous and noncommittal words battles the heaviness in the air. Storm clouds and the fog of memory bearing down on us both. But the half-smile that suits his face makes me sad. I want to trace the edges into happiness because they haven't quite made it. "Your good nature made you survive this long." I realize the truth as I speak it. Proud of him, pained for him. The latter the only familiar feeling.

This pride, this hint of happiness, this yearning from memory—it's only because, after a lifetime of our paths not crossing, we've finally collided. I've finally heard his voice. The space between us no longer silent. Every far-off moment and far-flung wish suddenly appearing before me, no longer unreachable but untouchable. And simply impossible.

Ding. The bells are still ringing.

When his lips part, he speaks, slow and serious, as if I'm the only thing that matters to him in the whole world. "And what made you survive?"

You. My chest rises with the truth, falls with my silence. Then, I speak past the silence. "My writing. I wrote when it hurt."

His voice of compassion fills my veins with warmth. "How many books have you filled?"

Unbidden sobs rise and I choke them back. "So many."

Another bell rings, almost finishing the farewell, the ceremony long over. The street is still quiet; the shop district stays closed on holidays, or mourning days. In the silence of stopped time between the bells tolling, he's closer.

I dare to ask. "Why are you here?" I think of the awestruck pain on his face when he paged through the journal. I just saw the poem in Father's journal for the first time, and now so has he. "What does my father's journal mean to you?"

"I can't say." For an honest second in time, his eyes shut. His chin dips to his chest after a shaky breath. No longer a prince, just uncertain. In this precious moment I treasure he must trust me. I can feel it.

I'm sorry, so sorry, for the sorrow filling his face. "Bells are wishes," I whisper. He lifts his head. A spark of hope. "That's how I hear them, every year." I speak to the sparking air; little does he know I'm baring my soul. Looking away from his penetrating eyes, I focus on the mourning flags framing his face in history. This moment I'll treasure just for *my* history, *my* memory. Oh, that my mind could keep this picture this clear. "Each toll must be a wish, because if it isn't—"

I must be mistaken, but his eyes are red-rimmed. "It's a curse."

A tear leaks out the corner of my right eye. I flick it away, even as he swipes his own eyes.

"I'm sorry," I whisper. "I thought I was done—"

"I haven't shown anyone how much this hurts—no one, except you. You think I haven't seen you every year? You think I don't remember who you were, that little girl who wept rivers of tears, who had to be carried away from her mother's grave by her trembling father. And then he—you don't think I remember? I carried twice the grief—" Unblinking, his serious gaze fixes upon me, speaking all I've felt for him as if he's shared it. How alone we both have been.

My breath catches, for me, for him. For us.

His voice narrows. "Neither of us is done grieving." I feel the air leaving as he remembers. Old fear, old pain. The daily overcoming. "They draw out the sorrow."

"Grief is for the living." I speak for him, sick of the drawing out of our sorrow in the streaming waters.

Heat from his skin reaches across the air to caress me. "Why does it feel like dying?"

Ding, dong. Ding—the final bell tolls. Cars start in the distance and commerce will continue. Life goes on. People will disperse, back to their lives and homes and families. All of us joined by memories and hopes, crushed dreams and hidden wishes.

"It's over now," I whisper. "It was so long."

A nod. A rod of steel keeps his spine straight as his eyes grip mine with forceful purpose. I need to know why he seems unable to say what he came here to say...wishing I could speak into the silence for him. Forever.

I close my eyes for a moment and make a wish. It's a photograph in black and white, the stark contrast of the past and present—or is it just him and I? Ever on the other side, always looking away. Never at each other. The most awkward, stilted, painful motion captured into a picture that tells a thousand words of our meeting.

Goodbye, dear Prince. I can never say what's inside my heart.

"I'm sorry," I say. I wished my whole life to meet him and now all I can do is leave him. My hair flips sharply as I rush out into the rain.

"Why are you—" his voice changes. "Wait, I don't know your name!"

He calls again, he calls for me. I don't answer.

It would be the first

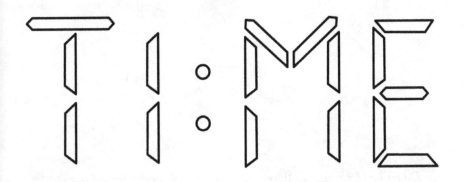

our parallel paths had crossed the
unsurmountable distance.
We are connected, but we have
never collided.

THE DUSTY
DOLDRUMS

December 19th, nearly 9am, many more steps across town later

Who answers a Prince with silence? Who runs away from a Prince? What broken-hearted, empty-handed young woman runs through the rain, without an umbrella, hair blowing wildly for only him to see? Gasping until finding crowds flowing through streets, black armbands pressing her in. *Tap, tap, tap*—my boot heels on hard ground, then softer dirt and side roads. Still running.

Me, that's who. And I have the distinct premonition it won't be the last time I'll run away from him. The question is, will I return to him? Can I?

I only had one wish and I ruined it.

"Look at your face." A lilting voice calls, then coughs. I adore Melody's voice, but I abhor when illness clogs it. "I can't tell if you're sad because you're soaked to the bone or sad because the weather finally suited the day." She has the grace to grimace at her own unthoughtful words. The sun had the gall to shine for a decade and half on every single anniversary of my parents' death. Today the rain remembered its fault in the tragedy that began my story.

Melody is a ray of light in the dark family dynamics of her mother and sister—my step-aunt, from Mother's side, and step-cousin—who treat me with ungrateful disdain and abuse my time and energy and finances to uphold our meager home.

A home I own, on paper.

Choked of breath, I hold my side, ascending the deck stairs outside our cottage, aching inside. "Not now, Melody." But the bite from my words isn't deep.

"How dare you talk back to me," she trills, attempting to laugh at her own sarcasm but just coughing again. This humidity always makes it worse. "Did you run all the way from the town center? Don't worry, Mother's resting. Get inside from this chill." She's one to talk, teenaged and pretty, but thin and not quite filled in.

She likely never will. Doctors can't pick a name for the chronic pain and propensity to illness that plagues the girl.

I collapse on the floor against the cottage beside her chair. The rocks lining the base of the house are cold. The deck bearing our weight but needing a new coat of paint.

"Two coats." I decide, closing my eyes and leaning my head back.

"White?" she considers, squinting at the faded wood.

"Yes." Window shutters rattle above me. The willow tree blows sadly, and so do the tall reeds at the river in the distance, though the harsh edge of the wind seems to have passed. I open one eye at her silence.

Melody considers me seriously. "Will tea solve this problem?" "Unlikely."

"Fascinating!" She claps dainty hands, then puts them back beneath her blanket. "Will flying save you from it?"

"Also unlikely, though possibly worth trying." For a step-cousin—such a mild title for a girl who's lived with me like a sister since I became an orphan—she's unusually attuned to my emotions. She's also good at brightening a mood. "Did you grow wings yet?" I ask.

"I'm sixteen soon, perhaps then?" Her smile is wistful, it makes me a bit sad. We could have been real sisters, in another world. It's difficult but not entirely impossible with her mother ever between us, no matter how we try to ignore her and live in our own imaginary worlds. "Bring those butterscotch candies when you make us tea," she demands sweetly. "Have to use them up before my birthday."

"Keep dreaming."

Melody's eyes follow the clouds like life, and her smile holds the key to happiness. Her calm is inexplicable in the storm of today. I want to cling to her and her happy possibilities, though I can't imagine what they are.

"Who did you meet today to bring on these doldrums?" she asks, too dreamily for my taste, making her plain black shift dress seem cheery on this awful day where everyone wears black, which is simply awful.

"Doldrums?" I roll my eyes. "Is that a word?"

"You're the wordsmith. Word-weaver? Spinner—no, you always get dizzy. Storyteller." She nods. "But you're probably a better baker."

"Don't tell anyone."

"Your doldrums are dusty." She brushes her lap, humming. "A dream is a wish your heart makes."

"Hearts can lie."

"Was that what today was? A lie?" *Tap-tap*, the toe of her lavender stocking.

I hesitate. "I met—"

"What a pause! Who deserves that?" She leans forward on her chair with her face between dainty hands. "Maybe a prince?"

I sigh, then sigh again. "I don't know—"

"Oh my gracious, it *was* the prince! Sounds exciting." Melody squishes her cheeks and overblinks her lashes. "Was he handsome? Such a shame royalty is only a title nowadays, not the absolute rulers they used to be."

"Really? What century are you from? They could have been tyrants, before."

She dismisses history with a flick of her hand. "Regent Garcon isn't that. His nephews seem nice, from afar."

"Go find yourself a palace guard." I poke her leg and stand.

A lovely hue coats her cheeks. "It's days like today that make me believe in the fairytale." Her wistful eyes trace the tree line. "That a king could save us all, and any girl could become a princess."

I can't deal with this. The Garcon family may simply be a leftover symbol from an age that has been slowly passing away into modernity. Monarchies are long out of good use if not fashion, and now, the Royal Family is a placeholder, ceremonial and fading from use.

But they're still important, and I don't want to dwell on it, because it still makes me feel small that Lady Garcon's death would always be remembered in a way my mother's would not.

A thought flickers from my encounter with the prince earlier. Of anyone, the brief unveiling of his grief feels like the truest form of sympathy I've ever received.

"Also, don't mention the war, ahem, the journal," she stage-whispers. "Can you believe I found it by accident while Mother got ready this morning? It fell out of her purse. I wonder what it was doing there, on today of all days?" she muses.

I smirk at her mischief. "Thanks for hiding it in my cloak."

"Don't mention it. Seriously," she closes her eyes, leans back, and pretends to soak up sunrays that aren't there, "don't."

"Would you like lemon or honey in your tea?" I ask at the front door.

"Don't deflect."

I smile, she wants both. She always does.

"I would *never*," I reply royally.

"You would always. Especially when your wishful, dreamy face is twisted with this haunted despair." Her charcoal smudged fingers fly in wild circles and vaguely in the direction of my head. "Good heavens."

I hesitate before going inside. After so long outside in the rain I'm desperate for the warmth of the fire, but I dread running into my step-aunt.

"Exactly," I say. She's always had a knack for emotions, like they were tunes and she could read them, though she doesn't usually come out and accuse me of feeling. My face must be a sight. "This is the problem with wishes," I mumble, and my arm feels heavy from my cloak—which won't dry for days—as I point a finger at her. "You have a hope and once granted, the wish appears and then, despair."

She smiles at my despairing description of this morning kindly. "Tea. Stirred with a cinnamon stick."

"Yes." I turn away, then slap my forehead. What with meeting the prince I've sort of loved forever—the same day my sort of evil newspaper publisher told me to chase the story of the royal family's supposed hidden heir, which will likely ruin the life of said Prince Charming—I'd forgotten. "Oh no."

"Here you go again."

"I forgot to give Azalea my work."

"Poor you." She sniffs sympathetically, "Azalea is nice but in a scary knows-what-you're-thinking-before-you-do sort of way. What is it this week?"

I can't help but chuckle. "A recipe for peach scones, and an obituary for the Winslows' grandfather."

Her pert nose upturns higher. "I'm not sure if that's better than the review of that film or your poll of pet names. Such random oddities Azalea assigns to you, *Rose Connelly*." She smirks at my pen name.

She's not wrong, because sometimes it feels silly to write whatever assignment I'm given just to fill columns in the Sunday paper and the occasional dailies. I've never turned one down, not one piece of work for a penny, all for a chance to string any set of words together. Someday, I'll choose what story to write to change the world. In the meantime, I must content myself to practice stringing sentences together.

Melody raises a brow. "How ever did you come up with a recipe if Mother never gives you access to the pantry unsupervised?"

"Midnight," I answer simply, and she snickers.

It wouldn't be the first key I've borrowed. Her mother is acidic about money, and with exacting persistence, monitors my cooking and use of sugar and spice, but she is often tired and tipsy in the evenings.

"You and me both." A finger flicks to shoo me. "Now, forget about your handsome prince," she titters the word, swallowing a cough again. How close to the truth she is. She has no idea. "Mother can be awful on a good day and this day is always the worst, you know that."

I turn the handle. "I can't forgive in advance like you do."

"Forgive later then. She doesn't have hooks or claws or talons. She has nothing to give, she's so trapped in her own pain. Sneak if you must, if you can. But you can't forever. The more we avoid the ones who've hurt us, the less human they seem."

I leave her outside. She has a point but I despise her words. Maybe I would be able to accept them if her mother only had it out for me, but that's not the case. Her daughters also suffer under her vindictive nature and manipulative schemes.

I step quietly into the empty kitchen. If my step-aunt knew about my meeting the prince, she would surely want to use my connection for all it was worth. Not that I know if the moments as the mourning bells finished ringing were anything more than a dream now past.

My dreams seem so much more complicated now that I've glimpsed one in real life.

I make tea. I wonder.

I only had one wish, and when he found me, I ruined it. He'll never find me again, and I could never go to the palace, asking for an explanation as if I were an acquaintance of the future king. Part of me wants to believe our encounter was as unforgettable for him as it was for me. Part of me just droops, rain-sodden boots and chilled to the core. Thank heaven for tea kettles.

I try stepping quietly back out through the hallway, but my step-aunt hears me from the parlor. I set the tea things on the narrow table in the hall.

"Where were you after the ceremony?" Vera asks in a quiet voice. I try never to think of her as step-aunt, or aunt, or family. In my mind she is simply Vera—a beautiful name, a hope that she's not all, entirely, inescapably evil.

My mind might be wrong. Her slash-angled form, tall with lips thin, shadows the opening between the parlor French doors.

I declare nothing with silence.

"Don't ignore me." Her voice slices through the air as her stiff heels tap on the polished wood floors. Floors I cleaned yesterday, now covered in mud.

"I was at Azalea's." Not a lie. "I dropped something there." Also, not a lie.

She's all raised eyebrow, downturned mouth. "It had better not be a valuable you lost," she practically accuses, and I shrug, half-smiling at her suspicion that frees me from my discomfort. I wouldn't believe me either. "You still haven't brought in what you owe me for your keep this month."

My ears ring with the warmth of anger. Loss of sound with the ability to hear. So unfortunate.

I shout with my stare. Face her straight, because I may only be eighteen, but I own this worthless home. "I'll have my wages soon," I reply.

I should've been paid today, but it's a holiday, and Azalea was with the royal court this morning or else she'd have found a way to give me payment for my last column. I fill however many inches the Sunday paper needs filling; they pay me in kind. This month it was a business feature, and that recipe and obituary. Often, I write what I know of the town. The people and shops who make the streets busy. The professors and students from near and far who fill the historic university, who make the air come alive with their questions and books. The grandfather grocers and lonely bankers and florist friends. Maybe someday I'll write about the royal family and the palace, Château Fleur.

I could write it all into a beautiful story, or at least, a beautiful article—a practical guide for tourists. I want to write my way out of this house and this story, so I'll keep going. And being beneath the blue-tinted air at the corner of Azalea's building today felt like fate.

Because the prince has returned, and like I always wished, he found me.

The clock in the parlor chimes the hour. First chime of nine.

I hadn't noticed Vera coming closer, today's paper in one hand. Second, third chime. I flinch before she strikes.

Making a wish never got anyone what they wanted. Having a wish granted was worse.

THE FLUSTERED
FLIGHT

*December 19ᵗʰ, an awful moment later as the hour changes to 9
o'clock*

"Don't lie to me," Vera hisses. A knock on the door punctuates
her slap on my face. "Keep quiet." Fourth chime, and then another
knock on the door.

Fifth, sixth, seventh. Silence.

As the eighth passes to the final chime, she calls out to her
daughters in a clear, guiltless voice and opens one of the front
doors a crack.

"What an occasion for a social call," Vera croons, but her excla-
mation reeks false, so I'm curious who it is.

In a flourish of rich mixed black fabric, Azalea Pumpkin sweeps
inside with a rush of wind, her plump face surrounded by dan-

gling, blue-toned jewelry, her confidence cooler than the rush of cold air brought in by her dramatic entrance. A trailblazing woman in her youth, she's been keeping the newspaper afloat while Finley ignored the business for shadier prospects. Shame he's the owner, but she's been my editor for a year, and I'm one of the blessed ones—younger staffers at our publishing office are thankful for her mentorship, hungrily learning under her astute eye for fixing wordiness with line-edits and identifying bad-eggs when it came to people. The latter was trickier.

Azalea is flanked by a bulky palace guard who squeezes in behind her through one of the narrow double-doors—we do have such an unfortunate doorway. He closes it politely, careful for one so imposing.

"Welcome to our humble home." Vera lowers herself gracefully into a curtsey, attempting painful regality in the company of the stately captain.

Gold-trimmed shoulders, stiffly pleated red uniform, multi-colored medals on his chest. Young and strong with eyes that never settle. A man to be beside in a battle. I hope he's on my side.

I draw away, cheek still stinging.

"And what is your name?" Vera asks, yet at Vera's cloying tone, the captain doesn't bristle. I'm impressed. "Can I serve you any refreshment?"

He tips his head to her, polite without showing deference. "This isn't a social call." Then he gestures my direction. "I am Captain Maximus Cavendish, head of His Majesty's Royal Guard, and I have a message for your daughter." His roaming gaze flicks to Azalea. "I've only just discovered her name."

"A message! From the palace?" Vera pushes Gloria forward. "We are unworthy and honored."

Captain Cavendish nods, polite, his attention briefly caught by Melody, who's snuck inside and meekly perches against the wall. "Your step-sister's daughter, who is your step-niece. You are her guardian, yes?" His guileless gaze finds me. "Miss Penelope Beaumont?"

Gloria blanches. I step back, nearly disappearing into the parlor. Head down, silent.

Vera's gaze pins me. "She is the eldest girl in our family." Her voice stumbles over the last word, she smooths the lace on her neck, dress severe and long-sleeved and *not wet*, thanks to my umbrella. "My *step-niece* cannot be who you seek. May I present Gloria, my talented daughter?"

Azalea regards her knowingly, then spins away from her to me. "Penelope, the Captain of the Royal Guard has a missive for you."

My eyes ping between them. It's a strange feeling, the captain and Azalea together making me feel less outnumbered. Like the forces in the battle are finally for me.

And suddenly, I want to win.

"Please," I say as graciously and unhurriedly as possible—a feat. I extend an open hand. "I will hear what he has to say." *At once, please*, I beg with my eyes, afraid to hope for two wishes granted in a day.

The captain looks at my empty palm and his eye twitches. "I have no letter or note for you," he states, and I raise my eyebrows. Vera gasps. Azalea, too pleased. Oh, the drama. I think my eye just twitched too. I meet the captain's eyes calmly as he continues. "Prince Nicholas says he requires the aid of a certain Beaumont young lady with a lace edged scarf and red hair and icicle eyes and," definitely a twitch again in the corner of his eye, and my goodness the prince—*Nicholas*, I feel his name sweep through my mind—remembers detail, "he mentioned she is one who seems fleet of foot." He examines my muddy boots, my flushed cheeks. I deny the urge to lean and admire my certainly wild hair in the mirror. He smiles broadly. "I'm pleased to have found you."

I shift my feet, a floorboard creaks. *The prince couldn't deign to write a simple note?* I'm not sure whether to be impressed or offended.

Vera decides for me. "You must mean my daughter," she says, "a true young lady of Loirehall. He must have intended for my Gloria—"

"He did not provide me a name, my lady. But I happened upon Madame Azalea on the way here, who informed me that this young woman," he points at me, and *my word* his arm is thick, "is clearly her." Captain Maximus is all business once more, any amusement at his description of me replaced with singular intent. He coughs politely into his fist. His hands are massive. He speaks roughly, but formally. "I must return to the palace at once, with her."

"The Château!" Gloria cries. She's the kind of girl who probably wished to be a bit of a wallflower, but her life and beauty—and her mother forcing her into the spotlight—has made her tough, harsh.

"Château Fleur," Melody repeats dreamily, settled on the arm of the couch, observing delightedly from the parlor. Afar, amused.

Maximus spares her a kind glance. "The one and only." He focuses on me again—my generally windblown appearance—restraint on his straight face until his lips quirk. "You may refresh yourself first, but then we must go." His smile is genuine, and

I can't help but smile back. *Of course* I want to go the palace, regardless of whether the prince wrote me a tome or regaled me with trumpets. I would come when he called. Maximus can surely sense my astonishment, but even more, my eagerness. He nods sharply. "I brought a car. I'll be outside waiting to drive you myself whenever you're ready."

I might clap, or faint. Melody wants to clap for certain. Gloria stomps to the dusty rose velvet armchair and flops, simpering.

Vera stands still. *Oh no.* Maximus snaps his heels and leaves. Smart man.

She waits until he's out of range to turn on her deadly glare. "What an absurdity." Her dark suspicion pins me as I feel my eyes widen, but I have no answer for her. "Whyever would the Crown Prince want a simple girl to call on him, to—how did he put it?"

"Aid him in a search," Azalea provides, too helpful, too amused. *The captain didn't mention a search.* But she's always seemed an enigma, and she's obviously stayed to finish this discussion for a reason.

I speak up. "Let me go."

"You shall not," Vera demands, her beady eyes latching onto mine—eyes too close together with too much space between the lashes. Gloria and Melody are both lucky they didn't inherit their mother's ugly gaze. "If you leave now you cannot return."

"You're the absurdity, Vera. She's been offered the empty apartment above my shop time and again, but she'd been staying here to help you and your daughters. When will you let her live her own life? Your poor step-sister—"

"That's right, my dirt-poor step-sister and her pathetic husband who soon followed her to the afterlife, left me with the soot-faced little girl used to too much free rein—"

"Not today, Vera." Azalea's voice is soft, like velvet wrapped around a brick.

At Azalea's admonishment, Vera stalks down the hall, single-inch, narrow twig-heels tapping but muffled by the gray-mosaic carpet runner.

"For you," Azalea hands a small envelope to me, eyeing Vera, a finely shaped eyebrow raised knowingly. "Not *you*. No more using her—"

Vera's hands lash, flinging like talons. "The girl eats food, does she not? I give her a roof over head and a warm bed. She must pay for her place here."

"In her family home." Azalea's wrinkled hands fold demurely.

"Our family strives together," claw-like fingers count off my sad life in the air as Vera stalks back, "struggles together, stays together."

"Because you overspent and left your family in this bankrupt state," Azalea's words are smooth and heavy, the velvet brick prepared to battle on my behalf. "You think I'd forget after fifteen years of watching you use her inheritance?"

"Take it." I pass the envelope to Vera. Larger bills—it's decent wages. If it's the price of smoothing my way out of this, I'll pay.

Azalea, a poof of dark chiffon to Vera's uptight and overly shiny satin, brushes me away with a flourish. "Go now, prepare yourself."

"What does he want with her?" Vera crosses her arms over her chest.

"If I knew, I wouldn't tell you." Azalea lifts her chin. "Surely the prince's business is his own."

"She's my *family*." The word ever pains her. I am glad to flit away up the stairs.

"That you would treat her as such," Azalea's voice drifts behind me, defending me.

I leave them to quarrel. It's the fight I've never had. What a strange comfort, to finally hear it spoken aloud. Truth long left unspoken, now wholly aired and deafening in ensuing silence as I prepare myself to meet the prince, Nicholas, again.

Stars.

Rushing through ministrations and the painful hair brushing I deserved after running through the rain, I dither over frocks. What does one wear when a prince summons her? Purple? Too royal. Green? Too cheerful, today. Black? Too obvious. White would truly be absurd, and I have no pink.

Bronze.

Well, it's more of a rust. But it suits my coloring. It's the hue of my largest freckles, too far from orange to be bright. The fabric's heavy enough to keep me warm. Buttoning brass clasps on the neck of my thick gray velvet cloak embroidered with doves, I breathe in stale attic air, feeling the silence, ready to leave it.

Finally, I'm ready to leave the dysfunctional home and the grim reminders of all I've lost. Finally ready to take Azalea up on her offer—living in the flat above her shop surrounded by windows and above endless books will surely help me heal from the memories that permeate the walls here, soaking them in sadness.

I'm finally going to try.

The house is cold as I leave, save for the warm grin Melody sends my way, sending well wishes.

THE LITTLE LIE

December 19ᵗʰ, precisely 10 o'clock, as the bells chime the morning hour

Morning bells greet a happy rhythm when I'm left alone in the middle of Château Fleur. Ten chimes where I stand, surrounded by grandeur of which I've only dreamed.

This is nice.

Evenly spaced brass sconces illuminate gilded frames. Richly lit artwork lines the walls of the stuffy hallway. Each piece is a person, the style aging as the nobility and royal lineage descends farther into history.

I look to my right. Big nose, jolly cheeks. To my left, an austere forehead, similarly black-clad in military dress. Kingly clothes for a line of kings. I squint at the gold plate:

Phillipe Leopold Irwin II Garcon, Duke of Carlingsen, the sixth King of Loirehall.

The last king of Loirehall, I remind myself, standing silent and alone before our history. Silent, alone—my history.

Heavy rugs with intricate designs mute my steps. Gold trims the far-up ceiling, and silver and gold brocade curtains the height of my house line tall windows. My *old* house. The cottage is no longer my home.

The stone palace is colder than I expected. There's a ten-foot-tall rectangular window, and beyond, a courtyard with two fountains, four cherubim, and green grass highlighting the gray of the Château's outer wall. White and light-gray stone, soft on the eyes but hard, so very hard. Surely that grass was frosted at dawn. It's raindrop dew now.

The bells end their toll. How is it only ten in the morning?

I wait two beats. Silence reigns at the head of this hall lined with oversized portraits of stuffy, serious men making me uncomfortable. Imagining their serious opinions about a girl wearing white brogues with a dress a lighter shade of rust than her hair, I stifle my awkwardness with a muffled laugh into the scalloped collar of my cloak.

"My ancestors amuse you." An amused voice shouldn't be so shocking.

"Stars!" I whip around to face the regent. The last living patriarch of the House of Garcon. "I mean, good heavens. No, it was the thought of my shoes—" My curtsey is deep and clumsy. "Your Grace."

Duke Erick lifts a tired hand and I straighten. He might have once been taller than me, but he's aged deeply, up close. "You are welcome here," he says.

"What?" I don't mean that, I'm just unsure how to speak. "Pardon me, Your Grace, but I'm not even entirely sure why I'm here at all." My voice drifts and his warm eyes hold mine steady.

A faraway look says he understands how it feels not to be entirely sure why one is anywhere at all. "My forebearers are here to remind us of how far we've come, and how the world has changed." He's lost in history. I don't want to follow. "We used to be the center of the Duchy; Loirehall, the light on a hill. As it was, as it should." His tired eyes lighten for a moment as he waggles gray eyebrows at me until I nod assent.

Loirehall became a constitutional monarchy when the duke standing before me became regent, but no child in Loirehall doesn't remember the list of Kings and Queens of old—I have distinct memories of being six years old in school and feeling terribly sad as a single tear marred my poor attempt at slanted handwriting, and somehow my teacher said the list was well done. *Well done.* That teacher helped me survive school that year.

Something sad in the air around this elderly man reminds me of that feeling. Those Kingdom Days ended with him, and these in-between days he's overseen as regent are nearing an end now too.

"The government no longer rests in a single hand in this state." Weariness weakens his voice. He didn't choose to be regent, and His Grace Erick Garcon the Duke of Carlingsen has spent his twilight years holding onto the throne until a new generation came of age. "We are but living statues of an older time. My nephew must come to life if we're to find meaning again. Purpose. He carries our future in his hands, so he must decide if he is to lay our legacy to rest." He pins me with a kingly stare, midnight blue drapes with golden tassels framing his ancestor behind him, highlighting his aged but proud stance.

His shoulders turn in, but he's still responsible for guarding the highest office in the land. His gaze, though firm, is kind. Green irises bright beneath bushy brows and the most crinkles I've ever seen around old-man eyes. He's got that hint of forest and escape in his gaze; it must be a family trait. I wonder if this life is what he wanted.

I lower my head. And like the noble he is—like the loving family he seems to be to the prince—I want to see his hopes come to pass.

"I did not intend offense," I speak softly, "truly, I laugh when I'm nervous. Your family has done a great deal for our country, for our people, in the past. What power you have now, what symbolism this palace and your roles carry into the future, they are good." I'd never voiced it, so I never knew how strongly I felt it.

But I believe it.

"Worthy words." He dips his head in deference to me, as if I've confirmed something for him. "But what makes you anxious, my dear? You are safest here, more than most places. I, for one, intend you no ill will." A caring twinkle returns to his eyes beneath thick gray brows. "If you give me but a moment, I might ring for tea to settle your nerves."

"You are so kind," I reply sincerely, taken in by the undercurrent of humor that seems a happy part of the nature of the Garcon men. "I wish I could bake you round cookies with the richest lemon buttercream to repay you. *That* would make me feel at ease." Then I realize to whom I'm speaking. I step back and try to sweep an arm gracefully. "I apologize, you must have matters to attend. Please, don't let me keep you. I'm just going to," I peer down the long hall lined with stern faces, "the prince's office? If you could point me in the right direction, the captain said he'd return for me presently," my voice drifts again, neither questioning nor certain, "Your Grace." I don't know etiquette enough but repeating that respectfully can't hurt.

Both our heads turn to the nearby voices.

Duke Erick smiles. "Enjoy your time at the palace. I must be off. I heard Azalea arrived and we have business to discuss." He walks away, dust motes dancing in the haze of brassy light.

How sweetly odd. The regent, so old and kind, didn't blame me for over-speaking. If anything, my unlikely manners made him smile. And that I could never regret, on such a sad day. It feels endless and strange, how much can change in a day, in so short a time.

I consider the extra-large painting he'd been standing in front of. The first king of Loirehall, wearing the pelt of a mountain lion and gold rings on every finger, brandishing a jewel-studded scepter, and bearing a crown that looks heavier, if you look closely.

I head toward the voices, down the long, empty hall. I walk uprightly, refusing to cower before history, before silence.

December 19th, just down the hall

He's serious. Grave, in a sharp black suit. White shirt, narrow black tie. Classically handsome. Tall, dark, brooding.

In a word, perfect.

Or another word. Irritating.

In yet another, *Nicholas*.

I watch from afar. He's enduring a long adieu from a group of what must be well-connected, important people. Each individual a jeweled card in the deck, holding on to the coattails of the rich Garcon dynasty.

For all their long halls of royal history, their future lies in the wealth of their ancestral lands in the mountains. Gems, rare-minerals, riches. They no longer rule—the Lord Chancellor of the Kingdom and Loirehall's Mayor, never mind the leaders of the countries with economic and diplomatic ties to our micro-state—saw to that. Decades of transition are finally coming to a close and still, the Garcon family are as important as the day the crown became a symbol, not a scepter.

Now I can see up close if their role—their story—is anything more than stamping laws into formal existence. If there is life and a beating heart beneath the formality of their status.

Over a tick of the second hand, Nicholas raises his head. His gaze finds me. Without breaking his speech, he satisfies the myriad of goodbyes, condolences, and requests. Suit straining against stiff shoulders, he's broad, but angled too accurately to those he speaks with. Precision and purpose, the performance of royalty.

It looks exhausting, though he carries it with ease.

Nothing in the distinct way he forms his words would leave anyone doubting his sincerity. It's a skill, to sound smooth and aloof—but still involved. They believe he's invested in their discussion and the only indication of his having any other thought at present is the straight lock of hair curving over his eyebrow, away from his otherwise smooth style.

My entire life has been like that stubborn lock of hair. It's no wonder I want to touch it.

Green eyes flicker to mine, bright. I hit the wall behind me. Can hair betray feelings? Did he hear my overloud thoughts?

In answer to my questions—here's my wild imagination flying off—he fixes the hair in a smooth gesture, never losing his train of thought. Proud forehead, dashing presence, he uses his other hand to indicate his guests precede him. Is that the direction of the center hall? The ballroom? I can't remember.

All I know is that it isn't even an interruption, this moment that made my heart flutter.

Fluttering inside can't be good.

Clattering, a pendant shimmers on the ground behind the exiting guests. Nicholas picks up the gold and silvery-white rose, tapping the shoulder of the elderly woman.

Ducking his head to her ear, his whisper incites her smile. Those must be kind words, spoken softly to have her incline her ear to him. Her white curls frame her sweet forehead. Eager to hear him, hopeful to thank him.

I watch with something akin to wistfulness. How often do our words find reflection on the face of those who hear us? That we would look more closely, or watch more carefully. What a story the face of our listeners would tell.

She pats his hand with her small wrinkled one, the kind of frail matron who only let life turn her sweet and soft now that she can't be strong. Maybe when you're old, that's what strength becomes. She isn't bitter.

Trust. Admiration. She cares about him. Whatever she says to the dashing prince, the straight lines on his regal face soften.

The owner of another booming voice appears. The wide-shouldered young man focuses on his prince.

What is his name? It is unusual, *oh yes*. Sterling Figgleston. Seeing him up close, his strange name doesn't matter. Any person who looks at a friend like that must be good. Sterling is all perfect white smile and smooth black skin, but it's his expression that reminds me—with a pang—of how Melody looks at me. Like a conscience. All tolerant raised eyebrows above an incessant need to get to the truth of the matter, or get things done, preferably on time.

I sniff but nod affably as Sterling acknowledges me, then he quickly swoops in to save Nicholas from another straggler talking his ear off. I finger the silk wallpapered white anemones as I remain plastered to the wall. Sterling is probably nosy like Melody, too.

Sterling directs the guests away and the collection of chatty people disappear down another hall.

Forest-green eyes find me. The *prince*. There's nothing wooden in their depths, only enchantment.

Stars! My thoughts. Then my thoughts remember how he said *no one, except you*. How can our parallel worlds come together?

Four long strides and he looks down upon me, ever the tall, dark, and handsome type to overwhelm an unsuspecting maiden.

"We meet again," he says in a marvelous baritone.

I raise my chin, direct. "You finally found me." I can't help repeating his words from earlier.

The fairytale forest in his eyes twinkles with promise. "I did." He scans around then starts quickly down the hall. "Come with me."

I'm already beside him, keeping pace.

"I have something I wish to speak about with you." Nicholas speaks formally, but it comes naturally. It suits him. "I am glad you came."

As if I had a choice—when a Crown Prince asks one to visit the palace, one visits the palace. "You had to collect me with a guard?"

"I sent the person I trust with my life."

Oh.

I count steps silently. The polished wood floor is seemingly endless. Persian rugs become black and white checkered marble, then a sharp turn into a narrow corridor lined with white wallchieres.

The teardrop star is everywhere. The decorative element below the torch-like lamps, the mosaic on the corners of the soaring ceiling of the entrance, even the connecting edges on the baseboards—detailed woodwork. Such quality on such a lowly place.

My erratic heartbeat settles in this quiet hall, neither stifling nor soaring. The corridor is as dim as it is narrow, but pleasantly so.

"No faces here," I mumble. "I can finally hear myself think." He peers at me briefly with a raised brow. I raise both of mine back, giggling. "Do you ever laugh? It was almost funny. Give me a chance! I was nearly overwhelmed in that other hall by generations of men wearing a starker expression than even you—"

He stops abruptly and I halt behind him, staring between his shoulder blades and at the straight hair edging his collar. Deep chestnut. Fairytale forests.

I shake my head; glad he can't see my freckles disappear into my flushed cheeks—*peach lost in winter*. I feel like an out of season blossom. Sigh.

In a flash, he spins and pins me with a glare. "You mock my family."

"I only mock the progression of fashion." I duck my head to hide my smirk. "I never said we were any better. Except the shoes. Definitely better. Give me a blue ball gown any day—"

"Do you have any idea where we are?"

I blink, detaching myself from his severe gaze. What have I done? Is there a code required to enter his office? Have I failed already?

"Château Fleur," I reply with a false formal tone, "built in the sixteenth century by your *noble* ancestors as the summer home of the king, whose lands were significantly reduced after the Wars of Religion and the Thirty Years' War but profited well during the Industrial Age." With an awful accent, I repeat the facts as I have every night when I couldn't sleep, which blossomed another one of Melody's unfortunately nosy ideas to find me employment. As a *tour guide*. Peach. Blossoms. I clear my throat haughtily. "Though neutral, these castle grounds were secret headquarters of Allied militia during the Second World War and were entailed upon the Garcons," ahem, *mister cardboard prince*, "and since have become the political and ceremonial heart of the region—"

Straight eyebrows rise high on a proud forehead. "You're a text-book."

You're a royal. "You're severe. What did I say wrong?"

Nicholas turns on his heel and heads for a single door. Knotted wood carved in an elaborate design, like a picture frame. Such abrupt manners.

I hurry forward. "Are we having tea?"

His hand lingers on the doorknob. "You have no idea what you're getting into."

"That sounds ominous." I pull up behind him, prepared to ask precisely why indeed he's ordered me to the palace, but the scent of winter spices and broken branches gives me pause. I'll decide if I faint or fall. *Or fly.*

He pushes the door open and while holding the handle, ushers me through to precede him on pearl-brushed marble floors.

It's sort of round, like soaring into the middle of a constellation and finding a place to study. I caress a set of gilded encyclopedias, one of many straight edges in the space curving around half the room. Every book spine faces the walls, only page-ends stare back at me. I smile at the cheeky books.

Then, I smile at him. "You probably call this an office?"

"What word would you use?" He settles his tall frame into a leather armchair studded with oval brass buttons.

I ignore the inviting sage green chaise and head for the enormous mahogany desk. "I'm not sure what to make of it."

"I doubt that." There's a smile in his voice though.

A wondering flickers through my mind about how many people get to see this place. Perfect princes only stay that way with a hint of hidden eccentricity. I know I'm lucky to get a glimpse behind the stalwart mask of the Crown Prince who exhausts himself by rowing in secret and has the physique to show for it. Here, I suppose, is where he has space to think.

I glide along the edge of the room, admiring the rounded ceiling opening with actual gold-rimmed, star-shaped skylights. Ivory walls with gracefully carved vines and ivy on the far end bracket the stately, heavy-looking desk, which has a backdrop of a brushed-white painted wall studded full of gold-glowing lamps.

"Starlit-library," I decide.

"There's no starlight in daytime."

"Is the sun not a star?" I pin him with a stare. "People and their prejudice."

"Did anyone ever tell you that you're—"

"Impossible? Outspoken? Disorderly? Definitely disorganized. Prejudice is refusing to recognize the order someone else desires, and I say the sun is a star." I pause at the desk. *Should I sit?*

An almost-grin. "I was going to say unforgettable," he finishes.

I turn away, fingers wishing for the spine of a book to hold for dear life. Except, the spines are all hiding against the wall.

"You are a very nice prince," I tell him, "but also strange. However, because you have need of a ladder for your bookshelves," I turn back and wink at him, "you are automatically my friend." He becomes rigid. I laugh. I've never felt so at home. "May I use this?" I settle into the high-back chair and become enveloped by the scent of lemon oil and shining wood smoke and stacks of new paper.

Almost heaven.

"No." He has to say *no* even though I've already sat. Silly prince. His glare is real but so is my delight at this majestic desk. Writing space. Thinking haven. He continues in that commanding princely voice. "And before you even ask you may not—"

"Yes?" I feel myself smiling at him still, unable to stop, my face oddly pliable. At once comfortable and surprised at my lack of discomfort. I wonder if that feeling will last when he finally deigns to tell me why he's summoned me.

"Never mind," he says, straightening to see my progress and relaxing again. Obviously, I'm going to treat every spare inch of this sacred desk space like it's gem-encrusted, and it's clear he knows it. "From what I've heard of you, you know people not just because you've been writing about Loirehall for years, but because you made friends over sincere compliments and histories shared over tea. No one can buy that kind of connection." He raises a brow at whatever my face looks like. He knows I'm an aspiring columnist *and* my awful pen name. "You're talented. You find the story where it hides." He clears his throat, and I feel it, the moment he condescends to get to the point. "I want you to write the story of my family, without embellishment."

My hands waver above the aged typewriter. Letters call to me to find their meaning. I can't imagine which brought me here, to him. Fate, destiny, all my wishes? I've never been able to find the one story that mattered to me.

Until now.

His attention returns to a gorgeous quill paperweight on the side table. "Please, say something," he pleads.

The letters, I rest my fingers on them. All the possibilities. But because of this morning—Finley's treasonous claims on the Garcon's lineage and the scoop of scandal he wants me to find here at the palace—I'm caught. Stuck. No matter what I say, if I say anything, it will be at least a little lie. I can't tell the whole truth, not if I want financial freedom from my step-aunt. Not if I want to get my own column, finally.

One way or another, I'm destined to write this story.

He's serious. Grave, in a sharp black suit.
White shirt, narrow black tie. Classically
handsome. Tall, dark, brooding.
In a word, perfect.
Or another word.

In yet another, Nicholas.

Two and a half
hours earlier...

THE MOURNING BELL

December 19th, before the mourning ceremony, nearly 8 o'clock in the morning

Rivulets of water were gathering between stone. The storm had come. I had hoped the start of today's story would wait for me to arrive at my scene before drenching me, but the storyteller had other ideas.

I headed toward the figure in the mist. I go when called. Am I curious? Am I willing to continue working for this sleazy business-man? *Has life left me no choice but to make deals with the devil?*

Dawn had already passed. Why did it still feel dim?

He leaned back, smoking an obnoxious cigar beneath the arch of the alley opening. Black armband already tied around one beefy bicep. Attempting refined in a full-length black coat, he looked warm and smug and too round to cause anyone harm.

That would be wrong.

A puff and the scent of ugly smoke overtook me as I neared, rain a living backdrop behind him. The chaotic sound a veil to the conversation I dreaded he was about to begin.

Augustus Finley.

My publisher. Owner of *The Loirehall Times*. A vicious editorial director and a terrible writer, he was also a cardsharp prone to believing conspiracies. Or starting them. How he hated when I refuted them.

"We have worked together a long time," Augustus said in a voice that made me want to check around my feet for dark, ghoulish things.

I have filled columns for your only respectable newspaper for years, and you pay near-nothing. Head heavy, I just nodded instead of ranting what would surely get me fired or my head chopped off; my neck already hurt. So much writing ahead of me, so much sadness. And the bells hadn't even tolled yet.

"Look at this." He handed me a folded slip of paper.

I hated being a fast reader—it took only one stutter of my heart. My gasp was covered by harsh wind. The storm seemed to want to tell me the secrets written in Finley's scratchy scrawl were treasonous.

"What are you planning?" I managed not to sound breathless from the fear making me this inhumanly still. Finley launched into a terse explanation of his claims, and I eventually had to interrupt him. "Why don't you publish this yourself?"

"Azalea is a thorough editor—the worst kind—she reads between lines and I'm not yet ready for my identity to be revealed." There was a proud tilt to the crooked length of his nose. "I wanted things to be different, but the prince isn't cooperating. If I do end up revealing myself, I want it to be with a flair. The coronation is coming."

Far beyond our clandestine meeting the mist hung its head, hugging the ground. Above it rose the pointed, sculpted tips of the old stone church. There was no sunlight to glint off the spires in the sky, but I imagined it would—I *knew* it would—on another day.

And that other day was all I could hope for.

How well practiced I'd become at that. Light, after dark. Starlight upon blank, black space. Ink spots on ivory pages. I would shine a light here, somehow.

Finley continued, "You have an opportunity to leave, to chart your own course. Won't you take it?" Sly words, so hard to deny. "I have a way for you to step out from your simple life, so just take the next step when it happens today—you'll know when it does." He flicked a pair of black leather gloves out of his coat pocket and smacked the top of my head with them and I felt my face twitch, so I bit the inside of my cheek to keep quiet. "I'll find you when I need to. Just do what you do best: chase a story." The start of a curve of victory on the mogul's despicable version of a smile was a sneer.

I didn't believe it was merely pride and power making him want to use me like this. There was cruelty, though I didn't yet understand what that malice had to do with me specifically.

I didn't really want to know.

But I would not shrink back. I would step into it because I wouldn't let anyone take it too far. I would prove it wrong. I would protect whoever I needed to. Who could I trust but myself—who else cared more than I for the fate of the Crown Prince?

"I will do this." I ripped the note into methodical strips, and Finley nodded approvingly.

Ashes from his loathsome cigar and shreds of paper flittered between us, and he crushed them with his shoe. But I wasn't quite his dark messenger yet.

"One condition," I said bravely, voice quiet, speaking to the stone ground to remind myself how to be strong. "I write the story." Whatever it ended up being—I doubted the question of royal legitimacy was easily answered. And if I had one specialty, it was finding the story within the story. That's what Finley could never understand. "Only me," I reiterated, and clanging punctuated my claim.

The bells started ringing, detached, trying to sound together but separating each chime of the hour from the other. Eight o'clock. The mourning bell was coming. We'd both be late. Finley stalked one way, and I hurried off another to the last memorial, the last prince.

Light, after dark.
Starlight in the blank, black space.

ink spots

on ivory pages.
I would shine a light here, somehow.

The Perfect Puppet

December 19th, present time, sometime after 10 o'clock at Château Fleur

Augustus Finley has ruined my morning twice today.

I focus on Nicholas' black Oxford-clad feet. "What do you want from me?" I ask the prince, dreading that it has something to do with my publisher, but not seeing how it could be anything else. "Why am I here?"

What story am I destined to write? *Must I write about a hidden heir? Does Nicholas already know of the rumor?* I lift my fingers from the typewriter keys. Heavens knows what I'd be writing if I started now, especially if both sides of this story are bringing me into it. I need more time. I don't really want to lie.

He lowers a hand from the edge of his straight jaw, deep eyes, so handsome looking back up at me instead of examining the marbled knots of the wooden paperweight.

A slow breath. His suit strains on tense shoulders, and any hint of give, any semblance of lightness in the air, is gone. He must have already decided how to survive his story.

"I know," he begins, "who you are. What you've been writing for the Sunday papers while I've been gone these years."

I frown, fingers uneasily hovering above the typewriter. "Do you have spies? Did Azalea send you all my articles questioning everything?" I mostly write culture and hometown nonsense, but I have been known to let *others* air their own opinions with a flourish in my articles. "Does this typewriter work?"

"Not for you." His low voice, cold.

The letters f, g, h, j—my fingers rest on them. All that potential. Words being stifled. "You want me to stop writing." My voice is empty. It sounds like he's started speaking words from my nightmare, my greatest fear.

Being silenced.

"No." Authority coats his voice as he stands. "That's not what I mean at all. I meant what I said about your talent—that's why I need your help."

I gaze up into a maze of green and hope I don't get lost.

From his inner breast pocket, he withdraws a folded paper. He extends it, his lean hand strong and wrapped in sinews, but there's a tremor.

I snatch the paper he's taken from near his heart. In two turns, it unfolds. With sharp creases overused from age, it's no longer a crisp sheet. The seal a golden star stretched, an ever-changing shape caught in the pull of another. Teardrops. A teardrop star.

The royal seal has always made me sad.

I cast him a glance, then focus on the words. Two columns, one old, one new with unfaded ink.

"What is this?" I ask, pain makes my voice thin.

My father's poem. *Passing Grief.* And *my* poem—my *additions*—with it, both copied in script not my own. I am torn, aghast. I am not past my grief.

"These are my words," I say, struggling to express myself. I wrote this just this morning, how could he—"Where did you get them?"

"I remembered your lines from earlier today, when I picked up the journal you dropped" he replies with a half-shrug. I frown. My father's work and mine deserves more than that. "I know the original," he says.

"Everyone does." The poem is an epitaph on the memorial by the Valais River.

In the weeks following Mother's death and Father's frantic, heartbroken, lost pacing, my father must have chosen to publish the poem anonymously, probably for my sake. Father never took credit, obviously not wanting to be named, so I never knew.

What I did know was that my father was too broken.

After realizing just this morning "Passing Grief" was my father's, it has made history look entirely new. So, earlier, I couldn't resist penning those new words with it. My father's good, kind words. A part of his heart fifteen years ago was anonymously shared for the sake of the lost families of the Yorkson Tragedy, that terrible flood. For the Royal Family, for mine. It fills me now with bittersweet something. Longing for happiness, yearning.

"Why did you add to it? Why?" he asks again. "This is your father's, yes? And you wrote this?"

"I didn't know until this morning it was his." I tilt my stiff neck. "How could I not add to it? I wanted to put it in the paper, to share—"

"No." Complete authority.

"No?" No to my poem, my additions to Father's beloved work? No to the past and the future? "Why not?" I know my words are good too; they are kind, like my father's. A part of my heart finally being shared for the sake of our families. A chance to give my father credit long overdue. "We are no longer lost children. It's been a decade and a half, Prince." That long since my father wrote the words used to honor the King and Queen after their black funeral. That long since Father's wife died with Lady Garcon, a woman in her confidence and part of her court, led with her to death in a car swept away by a storm surge. "Fifteen years and the words are now too much?"

"Because fifteen years without adding more to the story seems wrong." His reply is a dagger in my heart. I refuse to let his broken voice move me. Pacing away from me, he stops at the spineless encyclopedias. "Not with what I know. What I should have known I knew."

He's not making sense!

"What are you talking about?" I ask, my insides quaking at the sting of rejection. All the formalities for his mother and none for mine, but for this instant, I'd thought—hoped—that maybe this year I could have found something to offer for my parents' memory. And in a second, the prince seems to have discarded it and rejected me. "Why? Why not let me use my own words to carry on my father's legacy? To honor their memory?"

"It's personal." His tone is not unkind, it's half-hearted, which makes this worse.

I lower my voice so I don't erupt. I am a star, a supernova about to explode. I am a speck of light, fading in the night. "That is not your decision." I valiantly refrain from pounding my hands on the typewriter keys. My hands are fists.

"It is. It's private, and important, and I discovered something, so you just need to hear me out—"

"It is not *only* your decision! Are you so afraid of your own pain that you won't let me bind my own wounds? My mother died with your parents, my father soon after—do you think my pain less? Is it less important than yours, because of who you are? Who I am?"

My words fade. I'm standing, shouting down a prince from behind his own desk. In his study, in his castle.

On the anniversary of all this sadness.

"I'm sorry," I say simply.

He raises his eyes to mine. He'd been staring at the paperweight he held in his hands, but the near-black and warm-reddish hues spinning between his fingers suddenly stills. "You arrived in my life too late," he murmurs. "I'm sorry for your loss too." He looks at me with such compassion, yet a bitter root chokes the sweet—*I'm not bitter, I'm just sad, aren't I?*

I can't decide but also can't help but continue, still sorry for my too-fast words. "That poem was a spot of light in my memory, a poem written for my mother but shared for all, for her, and for the King and Queen." A twitch of his fingers, otherwise he and the paperweight remain still. "But now it's mine as much as it was my father's. He made me bear all this alone when he died. He's been gone so long." How stale the grief feels. It's just flaking off, and my voice is husky like dust coats it. "I only wanted to finish the poem. Make peace with it. Leave it."

"Believe me when I explain why I won't share it, because this *is* personal." He studies me, so I study his carved cheekbones and long unblinking lashes. Green eyes, that forest of possibility, darkening. "These words carried me through so much because I heard someone say them back then. *Before* the funerals." His chest rises, falls. "The person who saved me that day, he kept repeating one line. *Wishes for lost souls sing,* he'd said, after he fished me out of the jaws of the rushing river."

I gape, thinking of the epithet the whole kingdom's seen. *Wishes for lost souls sing.* Before, I'd always wondered where it came from. I hadn't known until this morning the words were my father's. But Nicholas...I hadn't known he was in the area when the water flowed over the dikes. I wonder if anyone knows this part of the story. It seems private, the rest of the tragedy overshadowing it. And my father had *saved* him. My mind whirls.

Nicholas must have a keen memory, to have remembered the poem from then, as a child.

"All my life, I didn't know it was you." He gestures to me vaguely in an offhand manner I deliberately choose not to be insulted by. "I didn't know the identity of the man who wrote it. I'd been kept in the palace and overprotected for so long. I was too young. I never found who saved me. But it was a kindness on the darkest day of my life and knowing it was his anonymous poem on the epitaph was a gift."

"I don't understand." My hand covers my forehead. I'm missing something.

"Don't you see? How else could I have stood straight to-day—any of these awful days for most of our years, but for his words. It's lonely." He clears his throat and I'm taken aback. Nicholas only ever appears austere, collected, but here, his voices catches on his raw honesty. "All their lives were unfinished. But now, your words make me want to finish it."

That's all my writing ever is—lonely and unfinished. What use are my words when none can hear them?

"They're just a wish," I say, leaning back heavily on the hard-backed leather of his desk chair. "What if no one hears them?" Emotion fills my eyes with tears, I can't help it.

He gazes at me kindly, not unaffected, but not taken down. "Why is that bad? Isn't writing the words enough? Isn't speaking the hope for yourself enough?"

Hope? Hope is silent. An unspoken word still a wish. But despair, despair is loud. Spoken curses in the quiet, shouts—

I open my eyes so I don't see Vera. Curses, curses can be hissed in the dead of night.

A curt nod, and he accepts my truth without explanation. He lets me struggle without making me rise. I wish I could. Because wishes, they don't need to be shared aloud to rise.

A wall falls, and his countenance changes. He comes partway around the desk, leans partly against it and crosses his long legs, bracing his arms behind him. "It made me less lonely, knowing you existed; that tragic little girl who lost as much as I did. That I wasn't the only one bearing the grief. Every mourning ceremony, every year. Every day." He looks at his shoes. "It's exhausting. I'm glad it's over."

I want to blame him for the death of my parents, but I don't think that will help. "I wish I could turn off my grief." How can I stop? I hardly could start—

Nicholas peers down at me, face framed by star-shaped window light from the ceiling, bright daylight breaking through leftover storm clouds. I keep seeing a forest in his eyes, moss ever lining the woods. But while I might get lost in the woods, it's so clear, I can't imagine not finding my way.

"I think you're like an iceberg," he says, serious. "There's so much more than the surface. And your eyes," his voice fades and he clears his throat and looks away.

"Are you always this direct? Is it because you're—" I cut myself off. *Royalty.* What am I doing here? What have I been saying? What has *he* been saying? "Are we in some sort of space-time anomaly? How are you sharing this with me? Why am I really here?" There's something in what he said that's drawn me in, some key. I'm tired and I'm sad. I can't find the right door in my mind to figure it out. "Will you tell me, now that my father's poem has truly bound us together in this tragic backstory and we've bared our souls?"

His lips quirk. *He felt it too.* Then a heaviness descends as he paces away again. No part of him seems able to remain still, not his clever mind or his restless motions. "You mistake me. That poem, that *journal.* Your father's death wasn't an accident. Because he knew that what happened to my parents—to your mother—also wasn't an accident."

My world just turned from black and white to blinding color. It's painful. "My father saved you." Breathing hurts. It's taken all these passing minutes for the fact to settle. I finally get it. The truth, that my father saved him that long ago day. "This is why you brought me here? To thank me? To churn up my grief just one last time? You couldn't have done that any other time in the last fifteen years?"

I almost choke but refuse to cry. Here I'd been worried about the scandalous story Finley has claimed about this royal family, but this, this is about *my* family.

"Only because I saw the journal this morning did I know with certainty it was your father who saved me. A person the royal court couldn't ever identify—he never came forward to take credit." A shuddering breath and his chest lifts. "He saved me, that day. I even remember this journal. It fell out of his pocket. He was so distraught. He kept saying it wasn't an accident, as if that journal recorded deadly secrets, and I have lived with those words this whole time."

He looks at me. Truly looks at me, like he listens to me—he hears. The collision. We are no longer living two different stories in two different worlds.

"You're his daughter." His throat works, discomfort and disbelief warring with absolute truth. The butterfly moment, the falling of the small journal from my pocket this morning. The intensity in his eyes robs me of breath. "He's the reason we survived."

My father, this prince. My chest constricts. Is this why Father fell apart after that day? Why couldn't he have also saved my mother?

"The dikes weren't enough for that much rainfall," Nicholas says, his spine stiffening as he turns away. "I was playing near the canal, past where you live, where it follows the road north of the palace grounds. That's how he found me; he must've been looking for your mother. But he stopped, for me." Nicholas taps books one at a time, not facing me. "You have the journal somewhere safe? Does anyone else know you have it?" He asks.

I nod once. Shake my head. "It's here." I respond, keyed into his tension. "No one knows." *No one who'd tell.*

Melody will keep secrets forever, and hopefully Vera forgets the journal in light of my shocking escort from the cottage to the palace. I point to my embroidered purse, which I'd hastily forgotten about after seeing starry skylights when I first walked in. The bag sits, smaller than the tasseled gold throw pillow it rests beside. It looks like it belongs. It looks like it might spontaneously combust, for all I suddenly knew.

"Such a small thing," he muses. Part prince, part philosopher. "All that mystery, our history," his voice fades as he talks to himself. "If he knew, he'd be looking. He must know who you are, which is why he sent me to you this morning, but he assumes you have no idea. His lies might finally cost him everything."

I try to catch up to his rapid-fire words. "Will you ever start making sense?" A thought flits by. "Why did you find me this morning?" I ask.

Nicholas continues, "There's something worth dying for. Worth killing for." The marvelous voice, the restless baritone, still confusing me. "I need to discover who is responsible for what happened back then, because I'm certain it's the person threatening me today. Not that there will be proof. And he will hold this over me, expose it all." His feet move him around the room, keeping pace with his wandering words. It's like he's forgotten I'm here. "It's why he wants to make a deal with me, as if I could lie, the rest of my life. As if threatening my brother would make me—"

"What are you saying?" I interrupt. "Expose what?"

Ideas keep crashing in my head. Father saved Nicholas. Someone is threatening Nicholas now, and that person sent him to me specifically this morning. Does it have anything to do with the story Finley said I'd find if I could get close to the prince? Is it Finley himself who's behind *all* of this? There's a thought, and one only I could have, and it doesn't seem a stretch, in fact, it's so perfect I want to banish it from existence. If Nicholas suspects I've come here with this sort of deception—

"I'm the lie," Nicholas says. "But I won't be a marionette like this." His voice breaks through the ties forming in my mind.

Taken aback, instant relief wars with looming anxiety.

Should I tell Nicholas? Should I keep up my own little lie, to protect him until I find out what's true? Do I really want to? How can I not, when my father saved him once? It's like I'm fated to save him again.

What will I do? An ugly feeling resurfaces, and it rings false, but I can't help speaking it. "You're the reason my parents died."

Our gazes break apart. Of all I could've said now, these are the only words I have.

"I'm thanking you from the bottom of my heart and you despise me?"

I gape. "These are manners?" I've always thought him a perfect puppet—without fault, without decision.

"You and I are long past manners." Restless fingers tap his leg as his gaze lifts to the ceiling, posture suddenly statue-like. "I want my family to survive my coronation. I never had a choice, not with all they wanted and expected of me," his tone is numb, "duty after duty, unwilling to ask questions but now, I want to—" life returns to his eyes and limbs. He focuses on me. "Never mind." He shakes his head, hair falling over his forehead.

I examine his prominent nose and proud forehead. But dark circles want to tell another story. I don't want to focus on that one—it might make me sympathetic—and for all that pleases about his countenance, I can't forget the painful depths his existence has settled in my soul. It isn't bitter, I thought I despised him, but this is something else. It's a black pond reflecting starlight. I'm not sure what's below.

"So, what, you want me to swallow this new revelation with grace so you can perform your duties?" I ask. "Are you accusing my father of something?" I close my eyes, holding onto the bright flashes behind my eyelids. Starlight, midnight waters. The prince's loss a mirror of my own. Every memorial a reflection of his life on mine. How I despised him. How I desperately needed to know another soul bore this load—he symbolically carried it for the kingdom and the monarchy, so I carried his.

I wish he knew how much I cared. I wish it was over. I wish I knew that he was doing this for more than just to protect his family through the coronation. I wish that for once, he would do something for me, and my selfishness makes me sick.

I close my eyes, so I don't cry.

December 19ᵗʰ, a breath later

I open my eyes to find him kneeling before me, stuck somewhere between apologetic and unnerving. Whatever he knows is ready to burst out, ready to change my life.

I'm not ready.

Warmth encircles my wrists.

I flick his firm hands away. Even I am startled at my exasperation. Nothing about him looks to force me into anything. "Don't touch me," I whisper, hurting like before, when I first met him. My heart.

Green eyes flash. *Hopefully his heart hurts too.* There isn't enough rain plinking the windows to fill the silence. I look down, trying to be ashamed. But he doesn't move away.

Another piece of paper slides into my line of sight, between his shined leather shoes and the marble floor. This isn't a well-loved note, not a letterhead nor a love note.

Ink bleeds through the paper. Soaked and weather-beaten.

"This is the same writing as ones I've received before," his voice strains to be quiet. "It arrived today."

I glance up, raising a brow. "It hardly survived." I don't pull away, my body selfishly responding to his nearness, warmth. Cold thoughts in my soul ignored at the very nearness of his face, his skin—

"It was left this morning on the outside of the car," Nicholas says. "Not here at the palace, but at the river." How can he be anything but a prince? He's so far from normal, he's extraordinary and gorgeous and intelligent—*stars*. I stop my admiring thoughts and try to listen. "In counsel with my closest advisors," he continues, "I have it on good authority that an heir of this position would be detrimental to—"

"Unless you're going to abdicate, you may need to speak with more plain language." I close my mouth, instantly regretting my stray thoughts and unfiltered words.

Why exactly, have I brought up the Abdication Clause? It is the most awful moment of the ceremony, to hear the old-timers talk about the previous Coronation. Like the awkward moment in a wedding ceremony where they ask if anyone must *speak now or forever hold their peace.*

Everyone hates that part.

And every Coronation since Loirehall's inceptions hundreds of years ago has paused at midnight on the winter solstice to ask a similar question. If the ascending royal chooses *not* to hold their peace, an irreversible abdication process begins, which in a single day—twenty-four hours to be exact—would dissolve the monarchy.

Nicholas focuses the force of his commanding presence in my direction, still very much the Crown Prince. Not shrinking back, I straighten my spine and push a stray lock of hair behind my ear. A lot of good that'll do.

"Read," he commands.

I obey and read. "Oh." I read it again.

The note says that the prince should find the girl—the description of me is unflatteringly accurate—who *holds the key to discovering the truth behind accusations against the monarchy regarding another heir.*

Lies.

Finley's found a way to get me into the palace and into the prince's private life by lying. I don't hold the key to exposing the truth of the rumors, except for the fact he's made it my job to find out. *Conniving publisher.*

I try to fit all this into my brain, and all I keep returning to is the fact that though Finley intended for us to meet to get me an exclusive for his treasonous purposes, fate had other ideas.

Father's journal bringing the prince and me together was not part of Finley's plan.

Nicholas is as new to the hidden heir story as I am—I just found out a few hours earlier.

This note...I know who it's from. I recognize the handwriting. If I say nothing about the fact that Finley asked me to write a story on this scandal, is that deception? Why has Finley brought me into this—though of anyone, imagining the conniving cat of a man as a usurper isn't a stretch of my imagination.

"Who is it? Did you know?" I ask, as if I don't.

He raises an eyebrow. "Did you?"

I cannot answer honestly, so I ask a question instead. "Do you know who it is?"

"Who wrote the note or the supposed heir?"

"Either?"

"I don't. But whoever they are, they want to bring down the monarchy. No," his voice hardens. "This person wants to end my family."

I remember Finley's words this morning, *I am the rightful heir to the throne*, and the way he shredded the paper into nothing, tasking me to expose the story. Hateful man.

I think of the silence of the judgmental rulers lining the halls with legacy, long dead. Do they tarry there with hard faces from the past to pull the strings of their heirs of the future? What good do

their manners and protocols hold now, with the world so changing? The prince before me often wears the same stoic expression,
until he speaks and comes alive. There are hints of living hope in
him.

I consider the Crown Prince kneeling before me. "Are we not
a constitutional monarchy?" I ask, though the prince knows better than anyone. He's more than a political puppet from what I
hear—he's unified council and politicians and diplomats with his
eagerness to modernize the monarchy and complete the transfer
of control of government from his family to the people. "Are the
assembly and council not now filled with elected representatives at
every level?" Inwardly I cheer my concise words and Azalea's mentorship as a member of the royal court. "Why would anyone want
to bring down the ceremonial part of our present government and
a powerfully symbolic part of our history?"

He arches a brow. "You should write *that*. But once again, I'm
not sure whether to be insulted or impressed."

"Both?" I shrug, then focus. "Does he want to preserve the
monarchy, this disputing heir? Or if he can't have the throne, no
one can?" I scoff. "That threatening note is a melodrama all its
own."

An almost smile again, and this time there's a promising flash of
straight teeth. It's the kind of hint one wants another promise of.

"You are just the right person to help me," Nicholas says. "They
told me you were like this," the smile widens another crack, "but I
didn't believe them."

"Believe whom? Of what?"

He shakes his head, taking the offending note back and standing
to tower above me. "You're staying at Azalea's bookshop?"

I'm afraid it'll be a lonely place, afraid I'll be a prop, abandoned and unuseful, instead of the star of my own story, always telling someone else's.

I sigh. "There's a flat above—wait. How do you know?"

He taps his temple.

I frown, then ask, "Maximus?"

He shakes his head.

Then a brighter, darker thought. "Azalea." Breath snags in my throat. "*She* probably started all this, or if she didn't, she has plans to end it."

A bare grin and a nod. Of course, the woman has connections with this prince and his family. The strings up and down, up and down.

He dismisses me. "I'll be there tonight, after dark."

After dark? Whenever could that mean? For all my propensity to delays, I like the idea of a timely goal. I rise and give my best curtsy. I can be graceful when I want to be, or deliberately obtuse.

"Should I make you tea, Your Highness?"

That smile. "Don't be late." And he turns to leave me alone in his office.

THE SPARKLING STAR

*December 19th, many hours later, nearing the end of the 10 o'clock
hour of the evening*

One can't be late when they're waiting, right?

I sigh, because somehow, I feel responsible. Nicholas was vague.
Uncharacteristic for someone likely more comfortable with numbers than letters. A time? No. *After dark.* How mysterious.

I start to unpack, moving into the flat above the bookshop just
like I've always wanted. Happy to be anywhere but where I came
from.

Up here, it's mostly windows and empty space. Pale floorboards,
white walls, one covered entirely by stacks of books in boxes.
No dividing walls and two entire outer walls made up mostly of
tall windows. I'll use the kitchenette downstairs and the happily
hidden corner bathroom up here that has been unused for years.

Cleaning unused things rather than overused is much easier. I give
the claw-footed tub a longing look. Filling that will take forever.

Dust covers a chipped white writing desk. A floor lamp with an
arched curve holds a shade four times as large as my head. A single
bed rests beneath floating webs in the corner.

How did I ever get in this mess?

Blessedly, a fairy left me a broom closet with—exclamations were
made—a broom, a dustpan, and a relatively clean stack of bed
things.

I will survive. As I had considered sleeping on my cloak, things
are already looking up.

I peek downstairs at the clock that will soon chime, then run
back upstairs and take a deep breath.

Cough—I attempt to crack open the only working window,
muttering about the point of windows at all when none of them
open. I need fresh air and dandelion breezes in the summer and in
winter, snow-hints and butterfly wings of long-awaited dawn.

I literally can't sleep without an open window.

Crack—it grudgingly opens the tiniest slice. And with the rush
of wind, a feeling like gratitude comes on the wings of a hope.
As if this story will turn out. As if this story will leave me in
wonderment, in a sort of throw-up-your-hands thankfulness. As
if this is a story to be grateful for, if I only keep writing words and
turning pages.

It's been two hours since the bookshop closed and I finished
my shift for Azalea. *Opportunity hire,* she'd called me. And since?
Waiting, cleaning. But ten o'clock isn't over until the bells toll the
next, and anything can happen in the final moments of the hour.

Like that feeling of being the last person to leave a library, time is funny that way. It doesn't let us get away.

Having finally tidied enough to descend into the dim bookshop and await my fate, I carry my candle and alight the stairs. Down down down. Leaving above-stairs for the bookshop proper. Mottled concrete walls are all whitewashed, better to contrast the gravitas of any book brave enough to be bound. And there are so many here.

Ebony framed black-and-white portraits line the narrow and rickety stairway, and a letterbox attached to beam at the bottom of the stairs is filled with forgotten papers—*I should look in there later.*

It would be spooky, lonely, and dark, except there are enough books with heroes to keep me safe. Their scattered and cramped presence up and down too-narrow shelves and enclave spaces makes me feel surrounded. A cloud of witnesses, a safe space. If I told them I'd made a deal with Augustus Finley, would they judge me? But I figure if I can't ask them, I can't ask anyone.

"How did I ever get in this mess?" I mutter.

"You unintentionally happened upon a state secret," says the voice of a prince.

I spin and my candle sputters out. "Stars!" Vanilla bean and cinnamon explode in my nose.

Nicholas swiftly saves my hands from burning wax. "Stars? The kind that twinkle? Sparkling in the sky? Falling stars?" Such an amused voice. Such a serious opening comment.

"Did you break in?" I didn't hear the bells above the door dinging. *Traitors.* They're supposed to announce visitors so one doesn't sputter in surprise. And I could have sworn the bookshop door was locked. "Was it not locked?"

"Answer my questions and I'll answer yours." He dangles a golden key between my eyes then pockets it. "Actually, we need to move away from the windows."

"Someone might see you with a commoner?"

"Someone might see you with a prince."

I roll my eyes. Glad for darkness lit only by streetlights through the curtain-less windows, and glad for new scents of earl gray and musty ink. Was it him who brought in the hint of bergamot?

"Not everything is that black or white." I'm glad I turned off the ceiling lights earlier. "Which is worse indeed," I mumble.

"I'm afraid I—"

"You?" I jump onto this topic that's been rolling decidedly uncarefully in my mind all day. "Afraid? Of a usurper?" Honestly, I don't know if I believe Finley is the heir he told me he is. After a long day of thinking, I've concluded it's more likely a distraction to sully the name of the royals. "This must be a stunt—surely you receive threats."

I follow his footsteps down the war history aisle. "Precisely. I know the difference." He hesitates between centuries, light from the streetlamp lost in the angles of his face shaded by books lopsided on shelves. "What they know and have threatened before—even when I was studying abroad—it's unbelievable, but probable. Even monarchs are human and make mistakes, and in this case, infidelity and secrets might be the answer."

As if I don't already know this. Augustus Finley has me all tangled up in it. I order my voice not to waver, even an untruth of this kind would ruin them. "How bad would that be?" *How bad is what I'm doing for your family?*

"I need your help. That's why Azalea and Max went to collect you, and why I followed you this morning, but then you ran away," he says. I click on a Tiffany lamp. Moody hues of sage and amber search the polished wood floor. He should hesitate more but instead he walks back to me. "Truly—you never told me your name."

I sniff, flip hair over one shoulder. "But you already know it with your connections." Azalea and her nosiness.

"What should I call you?" Exasperated, bemused. Emotions a normal human could easily decide between.

"My name, of course." It's a shame he's looking at our reflection, two of us between an aisle of books and the window. I want to look into his eyes to see what he's thinking and decipher his tone.

"I don't think it's your name." Taking the slim weekend paper from his jacket, he taps my shoulder, releasing a rushed hint of smashed wood pulp and fading ink. The column is folded open to my latest article beside a sponsored vendor piece about the flower shop. From the prince, I detect more bemusement, some frustration. "Rose Connelly," he scoffs. "It sounds like a tea biscuit."

If I had wings, they'd flutter. I also seem unable to decide between emotions the way a normal human could.

"Is that a bad thing?" I answer, imagining the quirk on the left side of his straight lips means he's enjoying this too. Part anger, part amusement. Annoyance at both emotions but a sense of magnetism that makes me want to dive in or laugh. "Sugar-dusted biscuits heal nearly all, and when they don't, tea passes time until we can."

That hair when his head tilts. "We can what?"

My desire to laugh fades at the sincerity of his question. "Heal, of course."

A hand on his heart. "You're saying it hurts because I haven't had enough tea?" He scoffs. It isn't rude, it's sincere and serious about the shard that, evidently, time hasn't healed.

I wave a hand. "Not enough tea with *me*. Or you might consider taking up poetry. It's good for the soul. Cleansing."

"Cleansing like burning, or like water?"

There it is again, his heart-pain that's survived the flames of grief and the waters of memory, never healing. Can we not have a conversation like normal people our age?

I shake my head. I'm eighteen and he's three years older, but talking with him is timeless and magical. "Starfire doesn't reach our skies for untold ages. It's cleansing like *time*. Time is the magic."

"Is that why you're late for appointments?"

"I'm not always late." I cross my arms, fingering the wide knit of my ivory cable knit sweater. "How do you know that?" I ask, frowning.

He still stands erect, but somehow more relaxed in his face, if not his stance. Crossed arms mirror mine. "Not from what I heard from your editor. I even met your publisher."

My arms tighten across my chest. "I meet deadlines." I extend the last second into eternity if I have to. Bits of time more likely to move than a deadline. "Azalea is the best in the business. But Augustus Finley is less my boss than the regent is yours."

A laugh that warms my insides. "I didn't like him either," Nicholas says, "but you have to work to pay the bills." I'm confounded by his shifting mood.

He's lighter here, brighter. As if being in starlit-dark brings him to life. It makes me feel like a star, witnessing his transformation. I can't even be bothered about his comment on my employment—imagining him worrying about income with his wealth is almost funny.

Browsing the literary fiction aisle, he wipes a long finger along the edge of a top shelf. He's tall.

"Dust." Nicholas huffs another small laugh.

I look away from his handsomeness, staying on the side of the classics. If Jane Austen can't save me no one can. These ones are collectors' editions, gift sets. If I owned this shop, I'd display these more prominently.

"What's so funny?"

"Your name," replies the prince, so close to charming.

"Penelope?" Somehow, I'm saying my name as a question toward the gold-lettered spines.

"Penelope." Hushed, he tests it. A corner of my heart tingles. Then, in a stronger voice, "my entire life has been so free of dust, from not speaking of the pain instead of letting it fall off."

I look up, his expression strange. Happiness and yearning. Is it a trick of the dim light or the dim hope inside?

From a deep pocket in his jacket, he pulls scattered papers held together with a slim golden string. "'Glamourous place settings, deadly cutlery,'" he quotes. My stomach drops. "Sounds like the start of a sordid story, not a fairy tale."

"It was a draft." I try and grab the stack of notes. "The start of a draft going nowhere. Nothing at all to do with my actual job."

He's annoyingly handsome like this. Brow raised, dark hair perfectly parted, brushing the side of his upturned collar. "That ending? It was terrible." He holds it aloft, unfairly tall.

"You read all the discards? From the trash? At the publishing
house?" I shouldn't be surprised he got into *The Loirehall Times*
offices. He's not just a prince, he's clearly on the good side of
Azalea—who's been a confidante of the royal family longer than
I've been alive—and because she's aiming to buy Finley out for
his newspapers, magazines, and printing business, she's firmly en-
trenched herself into this storyline. If that included helping the
Crown Prince with a tour of the offices she works as an editor in,
while Finley's obviously been away busy planning to overthrow
the monarchy, then I wouldn't be surprised.

"Your desk there is a mess." Nicholas' voice is almost teasing.
"The only thing worse is the overflowing bin beside it. So many
wasted pages."

I hold still, staring at hardback sets a long way from first drafts.
I can't attack the Crown Prince, not even to retrieve my unedited
writing. These scraps are the reason I've never been brave enough
to leave someone like Vera. What if I'm not good enough on my
own?

Instead, I say, "can you please give those back?" *So I can throw
them out again.* Such a falsely even tone, I'm proud of myself.

I feel like a jar of sparkles and if I get too shaken, bits of me will
go everywhere and never get cleaned up.

He flicks through the pile, stopping at scraps of paper in particularly terrible shape. "This one was better, the one about the
thieves." My lips part. His stretch into an indulgent smile, still
holding the odd assortment of recipes and lists and story plots and

opening lines that start in my imagination and end up in the bin. That story hook was my favorite, so I tossed it. "Yours, yes?"

Breathless, all these emotions fighting to leave my gaze narrowed in suspicion, open in curiosity, wide in shock. I shut my eyes and squeeze the bridge of my nose.

Measured steps sound away from me, down the aisle. I squint open my eyes as he deftly avoids lopsided stacks. Azalea needs more staff. But it occurs to me her letting me rent the flat upstairs for such a steal means she probably assumes I won't be able to resist organizing some of this. She's not wrong.

"Didn't anyone question your prying?" I ask. Somehow, I've followed him to the back of the store. Backs of bookshops and libraries are always haunts for lost stories, so I love them most.

"Look at me. I'm a prince."

I'm looking, I know. This dim light is more than enough to illuminate his chiseled jaw, and the noble set of his shoulders. It's infuriatingly attractive. "But how did you—"

"I'm far more interesting than I get credit for." Almost haughty, definitely satisfied.

"A mistake I'll never make again." I see that now. "And did you just *interrupt* me? Midsentence?"

Footsteps pause at the speculative fiction section. "You have no qualms about it with me."

I refuse to detect anything but distaste in his tone. He can't care or be amused or find any affection at all at how we interact.

I could never hold a shred of that hope. A ray of that light, one single crack, could split my heart apart.

He leaves science fiction for philosophy—the connection not as strange as many think—and taps lean fingers along another shelf. Finally pulling out a book. Plato. He brushes off the dust.

"Scraps of paper wishing to be bound to another." His words are nonsensical, but there's peace hidden here, between him and me and our dusty doldrums. He faces me. "Pens. That's how I'll call you," he says, smiling, nodding at my new nickname, not breaking apart our gaze.

I respond with a quiet sound, entranced by his smile—the truth on his face, light, and the crinkling around intelligent eyes—but having no idea whatsoever what to do about it.

My heart flutters then falls as his smile fades and the hands holding the blue-Plato-bound book clench.

Falling is always scary.

An awkward throat clearing. "I have a proposal for you," he begins.

Oh no. Of all the things I wanted, this is not it. I wait. I hope I don't regret not interrupting.

"The possibility of another heir weakens my claim to the throne. This threat is timed to not only discredit the monarchy but to hurt my family. Imagine if the people thought they'd had the wrong royal for a generation? What power the person with that claim might try and take." Earnestness heats his gaze. "And if this person truly exists and somehow proves it—and heaven forbid that person had tried once before to ruin my family."

My breath hitches at his insinuation that a hidden heir could have tried before to gain the throne by any means, and that the Yorkson tragedy could indeed have a more sinister layer of sadness.

"Do you really mean to suggest that the tragedy of our parents' passing, and the mystery of my father's death, are now caught up in a scheme deep enough to threaten your bid to the throne? That it's all part of the same story, or that it's the same person?" I'm thinking aloud, my questions as natural to me as breathing.

I don't want to consider that I already have the answer to that question. I rub the corner of my eye.

"I'm not sure if they plan to take the throne or try and control me," Nicholas replies, tension rolling off him. "I'm telling you this because, for all my doubts, the world is changing and this is me stepping into it, even if the council decides to end the monarchy within our generation."

My gaze stops at the mosaic of colorful spines before me, anthologies holding stories of any imagining, like this bookshop holds a myriad of stories—the stark contrast to the handsome, collected young man beside me. Gorgeous eyes framed by his pensive countenance. How opposite this bookish aisle is to the smooth, sleek lines of the hidden spines in his eclectic office.

He places the stack of my discarded writing on the poetry shelf. "Nearly every other storybook land and real-world district has moved on from monarchy. This kingdom needs to leave the past behind. I need to leave the past behind," Nicholas continues, fervent. "I didn't bring up all your scraps of writing to mean I didn't believe in you. You write well. Azalea said you could write a better story than whoever is trying to tell a different one." A deep breath. "I want you to write that story." His stare grips me, enchants me, grounds me. "If only because it's true."

Relief floods me. This is not how I expected it to happen when Finley told me his plans. His scheme to threaten the Garcon family with a sordid story of a bastard child denied a lifetime of their due. Nicholas hasn't told me anything I don't already know. But *how* he told me, and what he'll do about it...those are things a villain like Finley could never understand.

Nicholas can't be as perfect as he seems. If the world hears this, he will be unloved. Suspect, for the lies of his family somewhere in the past and branded a liar—the dark prince.

They would be wrong. He wants to tell the truth and there's nothing weak about that.

"The world is changing, Pens. You need to write it."

Here between bookshop shelves, specks in the air are lit from the light of a single lamp. Somehow dust always flutters, as if the air would be lonely, or bored, if there wasn't something dancing in it. I focus on the prince.

I would not cross this man. I might even fight *for* him.

"Please, say something," he says again, like this morning.

And once again, no matter what I say, if I say anything, it will be a lie. A lie that keeps feeling bigger, bigger. If I tell the whole truth, I might not have a job. Finley would end me. Without my column, how will I make money to survive? I don't want to go groveling back to Vera—the woman who already spoiled the small fortune left by my father and gave me none of it.

Now, there's a story. And here again it feels like I'm destined to write another one.

I wanted to leave my sad story behind at the cottage. I wanted to chase a royal scandal into the palace and appease my publisher and not get my heart entangled.

I can't decide anything staring at Nicholas and his earnest expression. Everything about his pedigree and his descent from nobility—none of that explains the look on his face, the tilt of his square forehead.

He may seem stiff, but his motives seem pure.

So just like this morning, I walk away from the prince.

I straighten the postcards on the spinner beside the window. Shivering, I ignore his reflection coming for me. Who knows who might be watching us outside? Loirehall is ancient yet modern, her people busy homebodies, full of life and as apt to gossip as to replant a trampled neighbor's flowers.

And it's chilly here now. The pendulum swings on the grandfather clock behind the till.

Tick-tock. Tick—

"Maybe we should discuss this tomorrow, it's getting late." I feel exposed, probably because I don't see how I can avoid lying about Finley's assignment being exactly the same story Nicholas has just requested I write.

"There isn't much time. The coronation is on the solstice. Either way, I am likely the last king. Help me make it."

Maybe I *will* fight for him. Maybe there's a way to beat Finley at his scheming.

Nicholas lowers his face to mine. "Don't turn away from me, from this. You cannot keep silent. Look at you! The story is already simmering in your fingertips." He turns away, pulling a pen out of his pocket and taking one of the postcards. "You're already searching for it."

"You dare tell me—" I lean against the counter on tiptoes to peer over his broad shoulder. He's writing a note for Azalea in crisp handwriting. "I'm a poet, not a novelist. I write columns about collectors and bakers and the candy shoppe on the corner."

"You write about people."

I give heaven—or in this case, the over-stacked shelves of books clamoring for the ceiling—an exasperated glance. "You're a *prince*."

"Is that not the same thing? Are you so prejudice against—" he clenches a fist. "I'm not asking for your help without granting you something in return. I promise to help you find the truth of your father's death." My eyes snap to his. He's deadly serious. "We both know there could be more to it. After seeing you holding your father's journal—don't you feel it? We share a story now. We need to discover the beginning, and I'll help you do that, if you help me find the ending of mine." He's intent on me, intent on my answer. Light plays under his eyes, lost in the dark. He leans toward me. "Penelope, I just have one wish. Can't you do this for me?"

I don't step back. "What if your story doesn't turn out the way you hope? Will you want me to write it then?" *Will* I *want to write it?*

"If it's the truth!" Exasperated, his hand ruins his perfectly styled hair. He's close enough I could reach out and touch it. Instead, my eyes follow his hand as it changes course, into my space. It never quite reaches me. He can't quite cross the distance—distance that's nearly gone. "You cannot be silent. You have to speak for them. For what happened. For me."

"For you? You turn your voice and smooth the ruffles of everyone's feathers but your own." I step closer, tilting my head up, fueled by anger and emotions I cannot yet name tangled in confusing roots underground—all kinds of sorrow hiding beneath. He drops his hand. "All these feelings, all this pain, and you do everything for everyone but yourself."

"Not this time." I can feel the breath on his words. On my cheek, against my eyelashes. "Not with you. You're different."

Tick-tock. "I am." I want my eyes to capture him. I may never get to see such beautiful eyes this close ever again. "I am different. Different from my family. Different from colleagues. Different from you." I am air and he is kindling. Perhaps the cinders will combust.

Then a flash brightens the storefront.

I feel like a jar of

and if I get too shaken,
bits of me will go everywhere
and never get cleaned up.

THE LOIREHALL TIMES

DECEMBER 20ᵀᴴ

CROWN PRINCE CAUGHT IN MIDNIGHT EMBRACE

Article and photo by Declan Hayes

HEARSAY SEEMINGLY CONFIRMED AT THE CROSS-ROADS OF CADLER AVENUE AND UNIVERSITY ROAD IN WRENLEY SQUARE. BYSTANDERS CLAIM THE PRESENCE OF THE CROWN PRINCE IN THIS, A POSSIBLE BLOW TO HIS REPUTATION DAYS BEFORE THE CORONATION BALL.

Photo: Final day of mourning marked by late-night rendezvous last evening

A decade and a half after the tragic accident where the King and Lady Garcon, and her lady-in-waiting, perished, Nicholas Garcon was seen with a young woman at the eleventh hour in what appeared to be a romantic embrace. The Crown Prince has just returned from five years abroad, where he completed military service after finishing his graduate studies in economics—a time with his own share of scandal—ready to step into his role now that he has come of age to become King.

It was reported that his confidant Councilor Figgleston was seen in the vicinity, and later that the Captain of the Guard was seen delivering a missive to the unnamed lady in question. There has not yet been time to contact Château Fleur for comment. Will this possibly suspicious coincidence detract from his finely polished public image? Will these turn out to be idle rumors of disrepute, or something more scandalous?

Crown Prince caught
in midnight embrace.

(Photo by Declan Hayes)

THE COMBUSTIBLE CINDER

*December 19ᵗʰ, a blink after the photograph, nearly 11 o'clock in the
evening*

The flash brightens the storefront. Blinding. Binding us in light,
warping our sight. My eyes slowly readjust, but Nicholas is already
unlocking the door and racing after the reporter.

Beneath my own cheerful tinkle of a bell, my hand hesitates on
the door handle. I'd started to follow, but then I saw who it was.

Declan Hayes.

This is someone I don't want to chase anywhere.

Nicholas is faster. He's already got Declan's scrawny arm and is
dragging him back.

It isn't raining anymore but the ground is slick, glistening with
the memory of it. I glance around, surprised at the pleasantly late

evening and the café on the opposite corner filled with a private party. It's a strange sort of balmy, nearly-winter cool. Bulbed lights on a dark green cord zig-zag through the far alley, extra tables and chairs littered around the corner. People in thick scarves are drinking rosy liquid from flute glasses, wool blankets tucked on their laps. Vivid colors and heavy fabrics and animated faces—tiny round tables between couples in conversation.

A crowd.

Nicholas notices too. He drops his hand from Declan but traps him with a stare. He doesn't carry the title of Crown Prince, King-in-waiting for nothing.

Nicholas. "Give me that." Commanding voice.

His eyes at a level with the prince, Declan just stares back without deference. He's gangly, but just as tall. He's Gloria's friend, hardly eighteen and paying for his studies selling pictures to papers, usually compromising or unflattering ones. Sickly slicked hair. Too much product, not enough hair.

Then Declan tips his head at me, smirking. "Hello, lucky Penny." Casual, proprietary, familiar.

"I am not your anything," I say, attempting a firm tone but taking an involuntary step back.

He may be scrawny, but he's strong. I'll never forget the way he aggressively, drunkenly—I cut off the memory. Who knows what would have happened if Augustus Finley—of all people—hadn't interrupted Declan's cornering of me in the printing room at the publishing house's New Year's party last year?

And Declan says he doesn't *remember*.

Nicholas' gaze slants to my shuffling feet. "Are you acquainted?" He only asks me, and it makes me feel safe. Like he'll listen to what I say.

Feet bump into the sidewalk. Mine. I wish I didn't get this sick feeling in a sharp coil on the inside whenever I saw Declan. I shouldn't have followed Nicholas onto the road. He's fine on his own. I shake my head once.

"Have you lost your mind?" I find my real voice. "Paparazzi photos of the prince? He caught you, just get rid of it. Find another story." My final words are lost in the air, though there isn't a hint of a breeze.

"I don't think that will help," Declan nods at the gathering across the square. Waving his camera at the onlookers, some are taking pictures with their own cameras. He raises his voice. "Well, Prince, care to tell us what you're doing with this lovely lady on a lovely evening? Something...lovely?"

Oh no. I gape at his rude innuendo. His ruining a perfect word.

Nicholas places himself between Declan and I, his body firmly planted in front of me. I let myself shrink, just a little. If I'm going to fight for him, I'm going to accept his protection when I need it.

Declan continues. "Penny, do you want a quote for tomorrow? I'll take this to Finley now. It's a compromising photo, so if you want to slant the story the right way, you should say something," his voice lowers suggestively, "or just come with me. Unless you're already dabbling." His conniving gaze flickers to the onlookers who've paused their conversation and lean to hear ours. His voice now sinister. Quieter, to Nicholas. "Either way, Your Highness, a scandal. Like your Pleasure Island headline a few years ago—that

went over well." Declan's words so full of insinuation, like he
knows firsthand, and I wonder if maybe he was there too.

Nicholas doesn't react—scary. I remember the last royal scandal,
there seems to be one every two or three years, but when the Crown
Prince was caught up in a nightclub assault case that ended with a
girl and a drug overdose, stood out more than most. He was never
a suspect, but that never mattered.

People can be unfair, even if they hear true stories.

Declan smiles shrewdly at what must be a wretched expression
on my face. "Like her father's death. Now the daughter of the
questionable columnist gets her own headline. No wonder her
father took his own—"

Before I can move, Nicholas grabs my hand, holding me back
with the force of his calm, the strength in his arm. I'm not sure
if he's protecting me from Declan, Declan from me, or me from
myself.

With his hand wrapped entirely around my own, Nicholas keeps
his steady, authoritative voice. "Spreading lies might get readers to
pick up your paper. Defamation and injustice won't keep them."
Nicholas squeezes my fingers, holding me. Holding me back.

My hand trembles in his. Startled he's touching me. Thankful
he can't see my lips quivering. I'm ashamed to be part of this, and
angry—heartbroken, pinched, hurt hurt hurt—that there isn't a
place in the world I fit in, where I'm safe. Not my home. My
not-quite-aunt deprived me of that. Not my work. People like
Finley and Declan make it toxic.

I'm sick of it.

Nicholas continues, "You don't want to go against me," every
word deliberate. Back rigid. I wish I had the strength to echo it.

Declan merely shrugs, stupid or brazen, and unflappable. "What will she do to you? Her reputation...the stigma has never left. You don't fit in, Penny. Too shiny, too worthless." The prince who stands before me is unmoved at these words meant to tear me down. I would be crumbling but for his hand holding me up, holding me together. Declan sneers openly now. "Get involved with her and it won't stop. I won't need to stir the cinders, like last time—old stories will come back to blasted life." Declan waves the camera jovially before turning away. "They will tear you apart," he calls casually over his shoulder.

Nicholas remains straight as a board, letting him walk away. The bystanders might think we've parted amicably, after that short exchange, and nothing about Declan's easy, swaggering gait seems to indicate the undercurrent of near-deadly disdain. He's crossed the prince, and I'm a target.

But I don't know how far this will go.

Crickets chirp for the second it takes for the crowd to disperse and resume their chatter.

Then, the first bell of eleven tolls. I shake my hand free from Nicholas, remembering with painful detail the way he looked this morning when he'd finally realized we'd been touching. I don't think I can stand that rejection again—especially not before the small crowd of partygoers across the street, only some more discreet and still others partially obscured by the miniature tree park in the center of the square.

They're curious, some slightly tipsy. We just performed the most delightful diversion for their evening celebration. Was it a birthday? An anniversary? A milestone with one you love, that's what they're together for, beneath the newly appointed holiday décor lining streets. Due to mourning traditions, residents and shopkeepers in Upper Towne delayed adorning their doors and shopfronts until after the December 19th memorial—today, finally ended—and now eves of brick awaiting the first snowfall are trimmed and inside scrubbed windows candlelight shimmers beside innumerable baubles sparkling amid multicolored fairy lights.

Winter's a magical season.

But then the second bell, the third, and I just feel more pain.

I move away from the prince. He could protect me from everything but himself. My gaze and heart and past all too entangled with his.

But then, he takes a step toward me. Gentleness fills green eyes, an upsurge of kindness. No pity, just understanding. I look down. Fourth bell.

"Have a little faith," he says. "You're afraid right now. I don't know why." He dips his head to catch my eyes.

I wish I could avoid him. I wish I could look into those eyes forever. I wish I could stop wishing. *Ring*. Fifth.

With the slightest motion he reaches for me. One hand, then the other. He moves the heavy knit fabric of my overlong sweater from my wrists, so he can wrap his fingers around my hands. The earth might as well have shaken. My eyes dart between him cradling my hands and the significance.

"I wish I could take it away," he says. He could not have crossed a wider ocean.

"I believe you want to fix everything." I want to recoil—from the possibility of pain, of the future at all in any form—but I am only taken aback and taken in.

Sixth, seventh bell toll.

For a moment, time stands still. And it is an earthquake. He isn't wooden, he isn't a prince. For this moment, it's just us, a girl and a boy under a starry night sky. Coming alive.

How can it be? Can it last?

A deep voice. "Who is this?" The question breaks everything apart and I startle at the eighth bell.

"Sterling," Nicholas breathes, relief evident in his voice even as he drops my hand like it's burnt him. All this combustible matter refusing to be anything more than a cinder. To his friend, "how do you always appear out of nowhere?"

Ninth bell and a bright smile. "Is this her?" Ebony eyes find mine.

I know him by reputation only, but up close he's wider and taller, and something in his voice rings clear in my mind. I don't want to shrink—I smile. Warmth returning to my limbs. No one has ever asked after me with expectancy like this, the kind that makes me believe anything is possible, or that I can do the impossible.

Ten tolls and another figure appears—the Captain.

"Maximus, where were you?" Nicholas returns to a stiff stance, shoulders straight.

Maximus gives a salute, but he hesitates. It's so short, I think most of the world would have missed it.

I glance sideways—Sterling didn't. But Nicholas is too concerned with tomorrow's paper, and I'm left standing on the sidewalk as he walks away with his friends. The only thing he leaves behind is a promise to be in touch about tomorrow.

Tomorrow. Strung lightbulbs across the alley start the starlit expanse early. All the glowing, and I'm standing beneath the unlit canopy of the bookshop where the Prince and I first collided.

I don't know when, but now I notice: I missed the final toll. The bells stopped ringing.

THE WONDROUS WISH

December 20th, not quite 11 o'clock in the morning

"Last night was a disaster," I begin.

"So I heard," Melody says, waving this morning's paper in my face. "Your understatements always fall short."

"It's not yet lunchtime. How much can happen in a morning?" My voice, it's whiny. "I'm sorry Mels, stop looking at me like that. I haven't had enough tea yet. What did it say? I haven't had the heart to read it."

Kind but mocking, she pokes my arm with the newspaper holding the column by despicable Declan Hayes that I haven't had the courage to look at. *Yet.* "Face the music. Reading always works out in the end. Just read, dear girl."

I slow my pace. Melody seems winded. "I'm older than you."

She hands me the paper, ink smeared on wet edges unable to escape the rain earlier. How I adored waking up to the sound of rain falling.

Melody tilts her head. "I can't believe he calls you that," she says, and I smile at the fact it took her the last five minutes to process the fact I told her Nicholas—*the prince*—called me *Pens*.

We've been walking along the edge of the Gray Forest. It's aging. Maybe we'll call it old, once we are.

I point to a nearby bench warmed by a lucky angle of winter light. "Sit," I order her.

She must be tired, for she obeys immediately. Wisps of thin brown hair frame her long face. She's willowy, but not like a willow. A willow tree seems sturdy to me—Melody seems like the sort of narrow-trunked tree with almost no branches that sways with every wind. Bends. Never breaks, her long fingers hiding her own secrets, just with pencil.

As providence would have it, I was already waiting when Melody arrived on the trolley earlier. She thoughtfully brought an aged, beaten cloth bag filled with books. It sits heavy on my shoulder now, but it will be worth it.

"Pens," my voice is wistful. Something sharp stings my insides. My eyes trace the audacious headline and the compromising photo from today's edition of *The Loirehall Times*. "He calls me Pens."

"Like the writing instrument?"

"What else!?"

"You're missing the amusement in my voice."

I ignore the paper to catch her dancing eyes. It's a whole waltz of hilarity, a swing of amusement entirely at my expense.

"I'm sorry." I sound contrite, but I just feel mopey.

"At least he was kind enough to give you a chance to talk today. Did he write the note in *pen,*" more titters, "or pencil? He must have a sense of humor, giving you a literal *pen* name and all. Oh, just look at you blushing."

Wait—how does she know about the note from the Prince his Captain delivered at midnight? I don't think I told her about it—or that he sent a pen with it. A slim black fountain pen with a flexible nib and fade-resistant ink. I'm not quite ready for the joke so I haven't mentioned it yet.

"Melody, I never told you, the captain dropped off—"

"I'm looking at the forest, the trees, the woods." She points fingers—elegant for one so young, though today they're already stained with charcoal—at the stunning view of the Château that I've been avoiding. "There's even a castle, modern age be forgotten. Something magical usually begins or ends in an enchanted wood. Especially in a place like here."

"Fine, ignore me." I ignore the palace and the paper just fine. "I'll find out all your secrets someday."

Smiling serenely, she stares at the woods behind the barriers that stretch beyond Cadler Avenue. They cut it back each year, but branches still emerge through the iron barricades, artfully wrought bars keeping the stone town from the living forest.

I'm undecided if it's trying to escape or coming to take over the town.

"I would go deeper, in the woods," she palms a hand to her chest, "were I stronger. I heard a story once in school that a skilled, eccentric carpenter built a treehouse deep within. It hides from those who don't deserve to find it."

"What crazy person would go off the path?"

"A curious one. They'd be my favorite."

"Melody Francesca Beaumont. The curiosity in your genes is going to get someone in trouble." I twist my hand in the air artfully. "Give me parties and dancing." I refold the paper, hiding my awkward future from my eyes. Not that it will do any good. "He doesn't know you and I are related. That I'm a Beaumont."

"Who?" she asks innocently. I swat her with the paper and she closes her eyes in an expression of glee before she dramatizes her questions. "It cannot be he? The Crown Prince who has finally returned? A *prince*? Is he a very nice prince?" She holds both hands up to block my next attack. A melodious sigh returns us both to glum reality. "Good thing Mother never goes near you in public."

I slump. "For once, I have to agree with her. I'm fairly certain he doesn't know we're related. I know we're not truly, by blood," I'm not officially adopted, Vera's guardianship will cease when I turn nineteen, so we are not related in the legal sense either. "You know what I mean." I glide the paper in front of my face as another trolley comes by, imagining the captured moment of time telling the wrong story of last night, though the closeness of the prince as he leaned toward me was something I was drawn to. "Who knows what joyous scandal awaits me at the Chateau. I've been summoned. Still, I'm happy we're connected."

"We're more than connected." Melody jostles my arm. "Someday, I want to be a nosy aunt."

"Truly. You'd be brilliant." I close my eyes at the warm, glory-filled winter sun-rays.

"Right?"

I spare her a glance. "But you sound wistful. That's my job."

"You're flighty." Nose turns up. "At least I'm not moody like Gloria."

"Yes, poor thing got all the melancholy." I delay having to go. "I met the prince's friend, Sterling."

"Oh, I like him! Such a sense of style. He's a bit bossy though, a bit of a know it all, like he gets inside your head—"

"If you like bowties—wait." I squint at her, and the sun. "How do *you* know him? Do you know the captain as well?"

"Oh, I just heard somewhere that the captain had joined the prince for his years of military service, and they were close, like brothers." She leans in. "But Sterling might help with my art. Sell my drawings for me."

"No!" I gasp. "I mean, yes! That's wonderful."

"It will be," she says, eyeing the sky. "One day, it will be wonderful."

"Are you ever afraid of how your story will unfold?" I ask.

Melody tuts, ever the wise soul. "Are you ever afraid a flower won't be beautiful? Do the petals disappoint? Even a rose in the briar, all afraid, isn't a thorn. It's still a rose, and it's beautiful. Give it time."

I adjust the heavy book bag between us. "How old are you, really?"

"You know how I dislike birthdays." She laughs, free as a bird. Flightful, airy, glorious wings. "It isn't my fault I'm like this," she places a palm over her heart. Sickly. Weakly. *Lovely.* "My body never seems to have had time to steep its own tea."

"Nonsensical."

"Off with your head!" She grabs the paper and mimes chopping the lamppost. "I prefer *whimsical*."

I stand. "I'm going to be late."

"Don't try to pretend it isn't on purpose."

"What are you going to do now?" I leave the offending *Times* with her. "Any parting advice?" I'd already explained how Augustus Finley and Nicholas Garcon both want me to find the truth about a rumored heir and how Finley's plans were thwarted by Father's journal and the poem—and how for now, the prince and I seemed to be on the same side.

I didn't mention Nicholas thinks the hidden royal heir could also be the person responsible for the Yorkson Tragedy and the death of our parents.

I haven't figured that one out yet.

Melody had laughed when I said I didn't know what to do. She isn't a fan of Finley even *without* knowing the one thing I do—he's the person with the claim to the throne, and he's shrewd enough to do something crazy before the coronation.

She grins, lifting a finger. "First, I'm going to find that tabby cat you told me about and rescue it and likely name it Peaches. And you: listen to Sterling, even if he's eccentric. Trust Maximus, he's always been a friend of the prince. And whatever you do, don't fall in love with the prince." She underlines her last statement in thick charcoal emphasis with her tone.

"Why not?" I ask, looking at my feet, wishing for it not to snow today. Ballet flats, black. My thick white woolen stockings. It wouldn't be good.

"Not, at least, until you've shared your secrets. Secrets grow in shadows. There are so many. Be a star, shine a light in the world. You can use this."

"What? How?"

"Go to the ball. Make the prince escort you—you're practically married now after that article." Her laugh is hidden, but her keeping it in doesn't stop it ringing in my ears.

I frown. "I could never. He's stiff and uptight. His heart is probably impenetrable and unforgiving and—" I stumble over words, the very thought, standing. "I haven't even been invited. Stars, Mels!"

"Pens, you know Nicholas." She holds up the paper, showing off the lovely photo—it's terribly gorgeous and romantic—shooing me off. "You're a thing now. And *things* are utterly unexplainable. What better place to try than at a Coronation Ball?"

I shake my head and wave over my shoulder, glad the sidewalk is empty.

Ding, dong. Ding—

"He gave you a nickname that suits you perfectly, Pens," she says to my back. "Tomorrow you shall go to the ball."

The baroque clock tower warns me the bell is about to ring questionable tolls over my life again. Eleven of them. I don't turn around, leaving tall trees of the wood behind and going toward the storied heights of the palace. I run to the rhythm of bells. I mean to be fashionably late, but not *too* late.

December 20ᵗʰ, well after the 11 o'clock bell
Amid the scents of honeysuckle and woodcuttings, we meet again in the open air around the corner of the greenhouse.

I speak first, tingling yet exposed from our conversation in the workshop just now. "Fancy meeting you here."

Halting strides end before me. With hands clasped behind his back, Nicholas bows regally in response.

I hold tight to control. "Hiding a secret? You can do that?"

I don't want to lose it in the northwest corner of Château Fleur's exquisite gardens. We both spare a glance at the parade of fancy cars coming down the winding drive, barely visible through thick trees. Shiny flashes of black through a copse of trees, people coming for a luncheon hosted by the regent, Duke Erick.

Wearing a suit jacket now, and suitably dressed to receive visitors at the palace, the would-be King before me straightens. "You're afraid." Keen eyes, wild-woods green.

"I am not." How does he hear what I'm not saying? I thought thoughts were meant to soar straight up into the sky, not stay where they could spill my secrets. "Why are you smiling like that?"

I'm already accustomed to the space in time he takes, calculating, processing. I'm not accustomed to this openness.

"Because you *are* afraid," he says, "and fear cannot exist for what you do not know. You can only be afraid of things you believe are possible."

Every second of my breathing shakes. *Everything* is in the air; everything doesn't seem impossible. I'm not afraid of the impossible.

He's right.

Nicholas holds my gaze until I'm distracted by a *plink*. Inky dots appear on the walkway between our feet. They hit at the speed of my heartbeat, plinking faster and faster.

Maybe I shouldn't have wished against snow. The chill in the air won't let this rain last long, and it feels like the precipitation is mocking me.

"Wait here." He dashes to duck inside the greenhouse and in my two steps following him toward the condensation-lined glass doors, he emerges with a tall umbrella with a wood handle and a bird's face.

Dashing.

That smile again. "Let's go," he says, and I take his proffered arm, grateful.

"I hate black umbrellas." I feel oddly hidden beneath the black shade. I've waited a lifetime to say this, this small thing that is so very large to me. The rain picks up. "It's silly, and odd, and weak to be afraid of the rain. I'm not afraid of the rain itself, but when it rains, I feel fear. All this falling. If one were afraid of the sun—"

He stops walking. "I wouldn't blame them." A gentler sprinkle, his kindness soaks my heart.

I can breathe.

Then, I can't, because the air between us becomes more. More more more. It can't escape—*I* can't. Beneath an umbrella, breathing syncing, our shared past and uncertain future between the negligible space between us. The lies that brought us together and the search for truth that could keep us—

I blink, gripping his arm. I look everywhere but his eyes. His hands are all sinews and callouses, not the smooth hands of a diplomat. It isn't fear making my fingers tremble, but the smallest hope.

But *people.*

His body is blocking mine from the view of reporters, guests, and dignitaries. Arriving in stylish droves, all coming our direction, opposite us on the path across the way, only a labyrinth between us. Knee-high hedges keep the crowd across the garden, but they see us, and we hear them.

Flashes of light from behind his straight shoulders. Glowing, bright orbs, capturing a moment. As if a picture could capture any moment with him, a universe of bright light and the dark looking for it. Hoping for it. Our past is its own darkness beneath the umbrella, between us. A world of our own.

And these lights! We chose them, too.

I finally return my eyes to his, suddenly rendered immovable at the single-mindedness of his attention. My voice is here, I find it. "We need to—"

"Why are we doing this?" His question isn't unkind or accusing.

It's hard to remember the reason we're doing this when he stares into my soul. I want to decipher the movement of his gaze across my face, but I'm distracted by this unusual curve to his straight lips. This smiling enigma. Victory now, but something else.

I acquiesce. "It's time for us to tell our own story, that's why we're doing this."

"Ready to be a distraction?" he asks and beyond reason, he's smiling for me.

I hear voices coming closer, the clicking of buttons, capturing photos in flashes. The tick-tock of seconds going by, time passing too slowly. An invisible pendulum.

Nicholas leans closer. "This is what they want," he whispers, then to himself, "but this isn't just what they want."

My heart floods as the air with rain, hopeful through the fear, at the vulnerable look in his eyes. Happiness and yearning, and longing between. The sort of look one has before they find a happily ever after.

I feel the moment taking me under. *This isn't just what they want.* "What do you mean?" I can only whisper.

Shadows beneath his eyes, but daylight. Winter sun breaks through the horizon and lights the air between us. Every raindrop shining like a comet.

A sunshower.

Is this the girl? Are you in love? Who is she? Are the rumors true about another heir? Will the coronation go ahead as planned? Will you bring her to the ball?

Voices carry like falling stars, but all I see is Nicholas. Emptiness is a prism, white to light, and darkness is only a space waiting for the light seeking it.

And I'm found, I'm found. I so badly want to believe I'm found.

"Don't look at them. Look at me. No," he takes my chin between careful fingers, "close your eyes and forget the world with me."

I try to read his expression and ignore my pounding heart amidst the sounds of questions about the scandal swirling about him, which now includes me. "You planned this?"

"Like I said," his words rustle hair above my ear—not that the onlookers can hear his hushed voice above the din of cameras and rumors. "This ruse is the only way. This hidden heir—who may be the murderer of our parents—needs to believe we're together and distracted." He's right about my publisher, the hidden heir himself, needing to believe we haven't considered a connection to the death of Nicholas' parents and Finley's possible bid to steal the throne. "They must believe we aren't near the truth."

On top of my hiding that I *know* Finley is the heir claiming legitimacy, must I do this with Nicholas?

"Another lie," I reply.

I don't want it to be for us, because this feels real, this magnetism isn't fake. *I'll tell him about Finley, soon.* My heart has never listened to reason, it's just full of wishes and Nicholas is before me, holding out a hope I could never have dared to have until this moment.

Another click. Another second. Only the unseen seems to matter.

His eyes search mine. "It doesn't have to be real." Like he said before, it's a distraction. But in this moment, that's not what he's saying with his eyes. Will the cameras capture that truth this time? "You just need to come with me to the ball, and we need to convince them you and I are real."

Your Highness, turn to us, we need a photo for the front page. Do you love her?

"Look at you," he says under his breath—*am I breathing?* "Now you believe everything I say." His eyes close for a second. *Tick.* "But you keep hearing the wrong thing." *Tock*, eyes open. He speaks louder, for the reporters, though forest eyes never leave mine and we are alone, deep in dark woods. "I do. I love her, deeply. With all my heart." Then again, in a hushed voice only for me, "all my heart."

Is this real? How can he mean these words? Could I ever believe them?

His hand moves beneath my jaw, turning my face up. There's a cleft in his chin. His eyes close and his lips cover mine with warmth. I called him stiff before. I called him uptight and impenetrable and unforgiving.

It's not him, it's me. I'm stiff as a board.

He breaks away, his breath quick upon my lips, warm in cool winter air.

One hand wraps around my neck, his thumb caressing my chin, his fingers tangled in my hair. Birdsong and the pitter patter of rain a rhythm to our eyes. Mine, across his face. He takes me in, one second at a time. A dance of glances. My hair, his jaw. My eyes, his lips.

"Isn't this real?" he asks. For me—just for me. He kisses me again, softly. Featherlight, flowing keys on a piano.

I don't pull away and he lowers the umbrella. The second I pause is an eternity of questions as winter descends and the raindrops turn to snowflakes.

Then I give in.

"Are you ever afraid of how your story will unfold?" I ask.

Melody tuts, ever the wise soul. "Are you ever afraid a flower won't be beautiful? Do the petals disappoint? Even a rose in the briar, all afraid, isn't a

It's still a rose, and it's beautiful. Give it time."

Fifteen minutes
earlier...

THE BALL BELL

December 20ᵗʰ, just before the 11 o'clock bell

The eleven o'clock bells rang twice through, each mark of the hour ringing twice as many times as they usually would for the day before the coronation and the midnight ball. I hear bells as wishes and so, from that moment until tomorrow morning—Coronation Day—every hour that tolled would give me more wishes than I ever had before.

Silly traditions.

Though, it made me seem less late.

Tomorrow, in the last minutes of the eleventh hour in the evening, just before midnight, Nicholas would become King.

I should plan on *not* being late for that.

The Château grounds were strangely empty. Inside the halls, the walls must surely echo with the bustle of staff preparing for today's other tradition, the Regent and the Crown Prince hosting a society luncheon. The press would surely come hounding, looking for the next chapter of the story the prince and I started last night.

First chapters are tricky.

In a poof of pine-scented dust and only a few minutes after leaving Melody, I bypassed the main entrance to the palace and stepped into the shed behind the greenhouse through the back door.

Carving covered counters display woodwork—so much wood—of intricate designs of tiny exotic birds. Various bird faces with mother-of-pearl eyes for umbrellas, or perhaps walking sticks. Melody would call it curious and delightful. There was something vaguely resembling a Nativity but with too many characters. Strips of shavings littered the floor, while a huge grandfather clock on the far wall was not yet oiled or ready to keep time or accept its timepiece—I vowed one day to have that in my home.

I set down my heavy book bag while scooting aside a set of toys, glad I thought I found a person—there was a dark head crouching behind the far counter of the workshop.

"Hello?" My voice echoed nicely in the low-ceilinged space.

A bang punctuated my question.

"My head isn't made of wood," someone muttered, then he stood.

"Nicholas?" I was stunned.

An expression I'd call rueful on anyone else swept across his face. No tie, no suit jacket, and his white sleeves rolled up to reveal corded forearms. One hand gripped a tool as the other wiped sweat off his brow.

"I must have lost track of time," he said.

My mouth wouldn't close.

His mouth quirked. "What is it?" He was relaxed, crinkles winking from smiling eyes. Hints of wood shavings floated in the light from many high windows. *The real him.* I was finally beholding the real Nicholas. His face was open like a cloudless sky looking at the sun. Its very own bright star.

My heartbeat was late. It went to him and considered not returning.

Nicholas set down an ornately carved music box with intricate floral designs that looked like lilies. I was momentarily struck by the thought that snowflakes reminded me of stars that reminded me of flowers.

So much beauty.

What is it? "Nothing," I finally said, then pursed my lips.

"That nothing was a book," Nicholas replied with a straight face, but his eyes were dancing.

I replied nothing. I couldn't lie, and he wasn't wrong. My heart had just sped through the universe and returned full of starflecks. And there was still a piece of sawdust in his hair.

Glowing, my heart. My mind unable to comprehend the perfect prince so far from put together. Scents of fallen forests, shredded strips of wood, and a spice like warmth swirled in the air.

"Pens, how do you know I wouldn't like your books?"

Stars. "How could you lose track of time when the bells are so—oh, why am I here?"

"I have a proposal."

I kept my voice from straining. "Oh no, not another one." Here I was thinking myself clever by coming here to admit to my deception since his first proposal was asking me to write whatever story I could find about the hidden heir.

I needed to tell him what Finley's asked me to do, or my insides might melt or freeze—whatever happened up there in space when a body was exposed.

Nicholas spoke firmly, businesslike. "We need to keep this relationship up if we want this usurper to reveal himself."

With sleeves rolled up over muscular arms, I wondered if his strength was from the rowing or the woodwork. Did this make him a carpenter of some sort? How well had his great uncle apprenticed him in woodcarving? What level was his skill?—*the treehouse.* But then his voice broke through Melody's story trilling in my mind.

"I've been silent for so long," he said, "it's made my life a lie."

"What do you mean?" I asked, hesitant, not because I knew that the very person who sent me to Nicholas is the heir threatening him, but because of the possibility Finley was culpable for some part of the Yorkson Tragedy. It was almost too much.

"This is me asking you to the ball," Nicholas said out of the blue and I balked at all the thoughts flitting inside. *Stars.* Me flying through the galaxy, wholly exposed in the outer reaches now. "You know, after they're supposed to crown me King, the thing with the dancing—"

"This isn't a joke," I whispered. This was the difference between the story I set out to tell and the story I was meant to tell—I felt pulled in two directions when I only wanted to walk forward. But how could he be this blithe when the person intent on discrediting his family might be the person responsible for our parents' death?

"I'm being serious," he said.

The meaning behind *serious* sparked through my brain. Part of me wished it could be true, when all he was proposing was a lie. A grand, sparkling, perfect lie from the most charming of princes.

"It's just for tomorrow," Nicholas continued. "After the coronation," he ran a hand through his hair and wood flecks flew off, "just make an appearance at the ball, with me." He put away his tools methodically, avoiding my gaze. "What if you're in danger, because whoever is doing this doesn't know we've figured out the connection between your father and me, between *you* and me?"

Clearly, he was thinking more quickly than he could speak, his mind processing how to manage the details, how to win. All I was doing was standing like a statue—the pretty, serene type with a dress that miraculously flows though it's marble—hearing him out.

"I think I know how to draw them into the open," he said. "I'll figure whatever else out, because if this person is behind it all, I have to—"

"What about your great-uncle?" I interrupted. "Have you told him?"

"No. Have you met him?"

I nodded, remembering kind, keen eyes in a face wrinkled from smiles. Like Nicholas a minute ago, not the intense Nicholas now.

"He's not made to be a regent or royal. He taught me all this woodwork, and even before the accident, he'd take me to the woods and build forts." More trills in my head about the source of the treehouse. I couldn't wait to tell Melody. "He's a woodcarver, but he formed me and shaped me into the man I am, though this life wasn't what he asked for. This was his true love and he left it to hold everything together until the time I could take over—besides, affairs of state are a solid matter of bureaucracy now. It's the end of an age."

My statue-self couldn't help but smile kindly upon the poor, worried human before me. Such a heavy load. "You will become King," I loved stating the obvious, "unless you use the Abdication Clause and decide to end it all tomorrow."

Solemn green eyes. "We have today."

Oh. I wasn't enough, or I wouldn't be, after tomorrow. Was he only faking this relationship with me for the sake of discovering the truth? Were none of these feelings between us real?

"What would I have been, in another life?" I asked, my heart hurting. "Your first choice? Your fourth or fifth? What value do I have? I thought you were a strategist, all evidence-based numbers and concrete truth—" I cut off my own words, because suddenly he was striding toward me with a purpose that I couldn't calculate fast enough, and I doubted physics was on my side.

"You have no idea." He broke into my space. Tall, finally the right sort of broody for the face that would suit marble. "Maybe I'm finally learning about the gray between black and white."

"Can I really trust you?" I couldn't step back—there was no way out of his space. *Unhelpful door* I just banged my elbow on. I hadn't moved my feet since first entering and catching a glimpse of him. "Maybe you shouldn't trust me, because now I'm here for the story," I tell a half truth, "my publisher—"

I didn't tell him Finley promised me the column if I exposed the Garcons as liars. I couldn't tell Nicholas, because I didn't believe he was a liar, and unless I did, it wasn't worth saying.

We have today. I would just have to figure this out tomorrow.

Dark brows lifted, but his eyes didn't lose the heat. He wasn't offended. "We'll find out who's threatening me, one way or another." Such a simple reply to the mystery nagging him, the one for which I had the answer.

I will tell him, soon.

"But if there really is an heir," I said, "I promise, I won't let that story go either." This, I had to be honest about. "I'm not doing this without a story at the end, but it will be truthful, on all accounts."

Now there were the narrowed eyes. "You threaten me? I'm offering you the world."

"For a day!" How frustrating! He was too near—I couldn't even talk with my hands, or I'd touch his torso and that would make me feel like a statue again.

"Then forget about tomorrow!"

"How can I forget?"

"Like this." He leaned into me. "You were my only choice. You were zero, before any other possibilities. It's a special number—it gives all others meaning and value." Green smoldering eyes wouldn't release me. A forest burning without flames. "That's how I think of you. Is that empirical enough for you?"

Breathless, my voice. "I tend to trust my instincts."

"What does your heart tell you?" Both our souls searched for the answer.

I wish for more of us. A time where every fear and sorrow would be forgotten. All the ashes, swept away. There would be no fires, no wood to keep us warm. Just light from the star and we would bask in the glow for a second and eternity.

I focused on the simple white buttons of his shirt, my eyes level with his chest, which rose and fell quickly, the only evidence of his strained emotions.

"My heart tells me to find the truth." I lifted my eyes. "Do you promise?"

"What?" he asked.

I couldn't deny it any longer. We had both been searching for it, and it led us to each other. "To find the truth," I said.

"With you? Yes." He reached for me, but I pulled back, remembering how he'd rejected me once yet also remembering how last night he'd taken a step toward me. The same kindness filled the air now, but it was laced with embers, sparking.

I wasn't sure what I wanted.

A shuffling footfall, in otherwise silence. But this time, when he wrapped his hands around mine, neither of us pulled away. He towered over me, hair falling over his eyes, looking down on me like I was the most breakable treasure in his world.

Once again, he crossed the oceans, the world between us, and the earth might as well have shaken.

"All I've ever wanted was to run away from the truth," Nicholas said. "I try and fix everything—but I can't. Not this time. I needed you. I need you. Please." His grip felt like I wished it would, and I wished he would never let me go. "Just for today, and tomorrow, stay by my side. We can fix this, together. This can all end."

For a moment, time stood still. And it was an earthquake. He wasn't wooden, he wasn't a prince. For another moment, it was just us. Staring at each other. Coming alive.

You would think the aftershocks of an earthquake would be devastating, and they were. But there was something about the dust settling, when the light hit it.

Wishes, that stubborn hope, possibility reborn, over and over.

And today I had double. I closed my eyes for a second and made a wish.

In this photograph, I wanted to stay. I wanted to live inside the sepia tones and unlike last night, this time, the flash of light wasn't unwelcome.

This time, it would last.

All this combustible matter refusing to be anything more than a cinder, finally coming to life.

Crown Prince and young woman
passionately kissing in the
garden of Chateau Fleur.

(Photo by Declan Hayes)

THE LOIREHALL TIMES

DECEMBER 21ST

CORONATION BALL TO PROCEED THIS EVENING AS RUMORS SWIRL

Article by Publisher Augustus Finley, photo by Declan Hayes

THE OFFICE OF THE CROWN HAS CONFIRMED THAT
THE PRINCE HAS INVITED THE YOUNG WOMAN TO
THE CORONATION BALL.

*Photo: Crown Prince and young woman passionately kissing in the
garden of Chateau Fleur*

Upending tradition, the yet-unnamed woman—rumored to be the orphan daughter of the lady-in-waiting involved in the Yorkson Tragedy, her father a former columnist for this newspaper—will accompany the Crown Prince. In the tradition of generations before, when the Coronation Ball was a large society event where a select group of prospective young ladies would dance a waltz with their beaus on a fateful night many who remember the Kingdom Days recall. They called engagement twice blessed on such an evening, when the bells finally finish tolling eleven, two times. But with a prince who discards tradition at every turn, it would appear times have changed in more ways than one.

High society and finery are sure to have their moment to shine tonight, regardless of how traditions change as Loirehall modernizes. The halls of the palace will buzz with such discussions on an evening such as this, which promises to be eventful.

The prince and Councilor Figgleston both deflected questions about the coronation ceremony and if it would proceed as planned amid rumors now confirmed by this editorial team. Much more important than the royal love story is the line of succession: there is a claimant to the throne more senior than the Crown Prince himself. Will the Monarchy survive? Who will be crowned King tonight?

THE TINKLING
TWILIGHT

December 21ˢᵗ, the next evening, sometime after 11 o'clock

"That kiss looked amazing." She's distracting me from my ruined dress, and I love her for it.

"Melody—" my voice can't be anything but slight.

"If you tell me your secrets," she's staring at me, nose twitching at the scent of burnt paper in my flat above the bookshop, "I'll tell you mine."

I try to smile, but my mouth wobbles. I finger the torn fabric on my shoulder, gauze floating away from the bodice. So much to tell her.

"Don't," her voice is sympathetic. She takes a fortifying breath. "Nicholas. He's the first person you need to tell."

"Maybe the only person." I breathe in Melody's strength, her hand guiding me around as she helps me unbutton my ruined dress. I wiggle an arm out. "The hours I haven't seen him feel eternal, but it's only been a day."

"True love." Her voice is muffled.

I turn back around to find her slipping off her ice blue dress and pulling on my velvet dressing robe. "What are you doing?"

"I don't know how Mother thinks it's okay to come and rip apart the gown on the date of the literal Crown Prince. She's mean, but even Gloria seemed taken aback, if that makes you feel any better."

"It was...personal." I recall Vera just an hour ago, pulling at my arms and lashing at me with her words. And Gloria, watching, not doing anything to stop her. I look for my reflection, but it's invisible through sheer curtains on the tall windows. I look down, fingering the soft material. My underthings are a dress all on their own, thick for winter, but soft. A gift from the woman who already saved me once today. "If Azalea hadn't come—"

Melody coughs. "Don't think about it."

Sitting at the desk, she finishes fiddling with the skirt of the sparkling blue dress she just stepped out of. Somehow, she's made the bustle longer. Capped sleeves and a glimmering undertone of blueish detail. A pearl trying to look like the ocean.

I come closer. The diamantes aren't round, they're stars. It's a gown of falling stars.

She stands and tosses it in my face.

"Oh, Mels, I can't." I clutch a sky full of stars to my chest.

"You can." At her forceful gaze, I toss the old dress and pop the whole blue thing over my head, and it falls in a poof. Then she spins me to fasten the pearl buttons all the way up the back of my neck. "Flying."

"Hmmm?" I try not to move.

"Falling is flying, isn't it?"

I think of whatever secret that's lighting her eyes on this dark day, the winter solstice. "You're saying this like you know it."

"If I did, would you promise not to tell?" She gently pulls the hair at the nape of my neck as I try to turn. "Stay, or this hair ends up twirled around a pearl, and that won't do when you're dancing."

I sigh. Quiet though, careful of the sixteen-year-old wrapping my décolletage in sparkly gauze. It's a bit tight but my chest is small, I'll survive. "You're giving me the clothes off your back."

"Not just any old clothes, this dress is something else."

I twirl for her. Pieces of glitter fall up into the air, and the bell skirt flares happily, trying to touch the floor but floating instead. Her smile lights the room.

"I'm glad you're here," I whisper reverently.

"Oh, me too. Look at you!" Then shadows cross Melody's normally bright countenance. "You should have left home before. Actually, it's yours, so you should have made us leave."

I want to stomp, because though I've been writing columns for almost two years, I'm still just a little eighteen-year-old not-quite-woman. I don't give in to my impulse.

"I can't kick out the only family I've had," I say. "And I wouldn't. I'm afraid of the unknown."

A pause. "Why?"

My words rush out because I've been holding them in my whole life. "What if it's worse than the known?" I sigh. "If Vera ever leaves the cottage, or moves away for whatever reason, I want you to have it." It's in my name. Technically, I own it. Not that it's ever mattered. I just think one day the owner of it will matter. "I don't think I will ever go back there."

"Fair payment, for a dress this gorgeous. I'll fix it up." She coughs again, collapsing on the bed. "I can't go today, not for the coronation. I might ruin the moment of silence. Need to skip that awkward moment without me making it worse. I can't hold my own peace right now." She covers her mouth with an embroidered handkerchief.

I sit gently beside her and rub her back. "Letters are important, they stand for something." We both stare at the elaborate red letters *M.C.* in her hand. "It's the Captain?" I ask. "Cavendish?"

She simply smiles.

"It *is* Max! There's a story I'd love to hear."

"You don't get to know every tale; I might just keep it secret." She smacks her palm on the bedspread. More glitter in the air. "You're leaving a trail of glitter. It's a sign. You'd better get going."

"As you wish." I stand, satin slippers slightly slippy. "I hope he can clean gutters and seal windows—the cottage needs fixing up if you want to spend the rest of your life secluded in an enchanted forest."

"He told me he'll repaint the attic and make it a studio. I'll draw until my fingers stop working."

"I hope you never stop. Find a way to keep the art alive."

"Your wish is my command." She trills.

I laugh, releasing the bitter feelings from the confrontation earlier and clinging to what's ahead. Every breath here filled me up again. I always wished for peace, and Melody seems to have found a way to capture it. She isn't holding it like the Crown Prince being coronated should tonight, no, she's pouring hers all out on me.

I hesitate at the top of the stairs. "Will you be okay? I feel bad for leaving my fairy godmother."

"Just don't slip, the snow might stick tonight." She lies back on the pillows and closes her eyes. "I wonder if Max's military uniform is navy or white tonight."

"I'll let you know." I promise, fervent. I will remember every detail of this story, so she'll never forget it. "I'll try to send him to you."

"He's busy today." Love fills her voice, love that second story windows and the long walk to the church can't possibly contain. He'll come for her.

"That captain will find a way to check on you. However did you meet him?" I wonder aloud.

"Destiny never tells." She sighs dreamily. "The bells are going to ring. You must go."

Behind the sheers is a blackening sky, so I squint for unseen starlight through the window. Streetlamps block the view, and my breath fogs the glass.

"The biggest star you see isn't necessarily the closest," she says. "I like this, the sparkling and light dancing on sweet things."

I smile, because she's trying so hard to make me smile. Then we're both silenced.

Ding, breathe. *Dong*.

The bells. I'm late.

I'm about to pick up my dress and take off down the stairs in my slippers when another set of bells ring cheerily in the frosty air.

The trolley.

I return to the window at the top of the stairs.

"He made it." Melody's soft voice, farther away than it should have seemed.

"Who?" I ask. A boy, a young man really, leans out the driver's window. Overlong dark hair curls mischievously above the filigreed collar of his royal coat. "That's not Max."

A muffled laugh. I check on her. Her face is buried in the pillow.

"He said he'd help somehow even though he's busy. He obviously sent a substitute. Another character in our wild story."

"Obviously. Captain of the Guard and all."

"Yes, he is."

"Listen to you swooning, good thing you're lying down." I smile and grasp the smooth handle of the railing. "You'll tell me later, about you and him?" I pause at the top of the stairs. "Does your mother know? Are you hiding your true love because she'd have a fit?"

"I'll have a fit if you're late, be gone with you."

"This is crazy."

More sleepy laughs. "So is a midnight coronation, who are we to change the story?"

I rush down, ignoring her amused mumbling about knowing how I'd end up being late.

The boy waves and I dash down the street to meet him. "Who are you?"

"My brother and Max sent me," the young man says—*what a fascinating grin*. I see it now, familiar woods of enchantment in these young eyes.

But Nicholas' younger brother Pierre's eyes spark with a darker shadow. He's trouble and unafraid of doing anything for his family.

"I couldn't imagine anything better," I respond sincerely.

He tips cheeky fingers against his military style hat as I gingerly climb in. I gasp and barely hold on as he gets the trolley in motion up the slight incline. I can't help but smile.

"How do you know how to drive this? Never mind," I shake my head and thankfully, no hair gets stuck in the pearls. "I don't want to know."

"I like you already," he says. "You're late already, but I get that, it's a family trait for us too. You can't imagine what my brother is like without Sterling." Mischief cackles. "But I know a side entrance. You can watch without being seen. This is the best way."

How a voice calling above the wind can be so nostalgic makes me smile as he continues, as if he's giving me the royal trolley tour, which isn't a thing but with him could be. "You know what my great-uncle used to say, before he became regent and serious all the time? 'Someday the tides will turn, the wind will change, the seas will calm. Until then, paddle like crazy!'" Pierre laughs, free and easy and unburdened, speeding us along, as though escaping the shadows trying to claim the bright in his eyes. "Let's fly!"

I laugh with him, thinking he'll make a wonderful father someday. Once he grows up.

THE MANGLED MIDNIGHT

December 21ˢᵗ, almost 12 o'clock, nearing the midnight Coronation ceremony

Nicholas hasn't seen me. He's alone, in black military dress. All gold accents and strong stature, decorations of valor, all symbols of history he deserves to bear. Rich buttons, a red sash, and a studded belt.

Nothing is being held together. It's all falling apart.

My heart wanders and though I've tried to sneak in a hidden side door down a dark hallway, I've instead come across the moment that defines my life.

My feet stop in a whisper at this accident. The shocking moment of heartbreak making time stop when I can't hold on.

Nicholas, the Crown Prince of Loirehall, thinks he's alone. His head drops heavily, shoulders shaking.

Time makes me watch in the agony of a second. That most awful endlessness it takes for the first tear to break through, the buildup and burn until there's a single quiver of his jaw, then—

Tears. Falling falling falling.

At first, his eyes are closed and it's a quiet heartbreaking.

He doesn't know where to look, a step here, pacing there. Nowhere can take him away from this. Uneven breaths as he looks up at the clustered ceiling, at one wall with twin dim lamps then to the opposite wall adorned in a historical monument to paint colored in arcing motifs of history, sacrifice, and truth.

Truth.

The prince, without peace, broken before me. His tears, falling. My heart, torn.

I'd come here hoping to tell the truth, but here I am finding it. Strange, to be first to witness the twilight of an era, and the ending of the monarchy. Amid the glory of ancestors, he should be king.

But that is not our future.

His breath shudders, a hand covering his mouth. With the other, he pulls off his peak cap hat, black with gold teardrop stars, every emblem embroidered to perfection. Loirehall and her history, falling away. Held together on him, for only he can let it go.

My ribs hurt at the strain in his face. He'd left the door ajar; my presence is unnoticed until an arc of starry pearls trace constellations across the cold stone floor. Even the heavens are cold. Melody's borrowed dress reflects showers as specks of beauty on the floor beneath our feet, catching his teardrops.

We notice the light together. I cover my mouth as he turns to me.

The agony painted across his face propels me forward. "I'm sorry," I say, appalled when he steps back. Away.

He wipes wetness from his cheek. Looking down, deep lines on his forehead, his mouth twists as tears leave another trail beside it. He swallows thickly, breathing out.

My voice catches at this sight of him. I've held a candle for him in my heart for years. But like this?

"I was late," I try again.

He sniffs, a painful huff to control the shaking. "So am I. Late. We're similar." A harsher laugh as his eyes sweep over me.

But then his tone settles in my mind. An unmistakable echo after words ring then fade into silence.

Lies.

"You already knew," I whisper. He knew that I'd been working for Finley all along. He did this all with me anyway, because he'd already decided to give up the throne. I breathe—I can't breathe. "You don't have to do this."

He takes another step back, muffling his hair in agitation. Perfectly shined shoes. I can't let him back away, and I can't let him go. Not before I tell him the most important truth, when he clearly knows the *next* important truth.

"Your face," he says roughly. Like ripped velvet, harsh doesn't suit his usually smooth baritone. "Somebody didn't have enough tea this morning. You couldn't even attend promptly the coronation of the prince you're pretending to love?" His words slice strings of my heart. "Or have you just been waiting for the best moment to take me down?"

"The world could always use more tea," I reply automatically, my last cup of calming tea so very long ago, refusing to let the frayed edges of my heart believe his words.

I won't turn away from his piercing gaze and the memory branded in my mind of the fringed epaulette on his shoulders shaking with the true depth of his sorrow when he thought no one could see him.

I step across the chill of echoing, cold stone reflecting my dress's diamonds, walking across the heavens for him.

I would cross all the stars of the universe for him.

I wish he knew this one truth. "I love you." Wild words, for wild times.

Disbelief as his lips part and the formal cast of his tall frame cracks. "You're bold. I'll give you that. I almost believe—"

"It's true. And there's more, more I need to tell you." I pause, unsure how to begin untangling the truth from the lies in our lives.

"Do you know why tea is important?" he asks, as if his coronation isn't around the literal corner in this dim vestry of the historic stone church.

As if we're not both already too late.

I have no words. This is absurd.

He gazes at me, once again collected. "Tea means you're sitting down. It means you talk. And people who sit down make the world a better place than those who don't, because they listen." This is no calm. His soft words are fearfully forceful. "What is there to celebrate, this evil day? Where are the messengers of peace? It's all ill news and dark omens. A past that couldn't stay buried." His straight bearing is so regal, so business-like, so heartbreaking. "It's Finley. But you knew that already, didn't you?"

"I'm sorry," I breathe. Finley must have given up on me and gone straight to the prince this time, twisting my role, making Nicholas doubt me. But I need Nicholas to know I never would have given up on him. "I should have told you before that I knew Finley was the hidden heir and that he'd given me the story."

"Why are you sorry? This isn't your lie. The lie is standing right in front of you." His hands brush down his black coat, pitch-dark hair styled crisp and perfect. "I represent the life that was ripped away from you. I took everything away from you. It's my fault. If not for my family, your parents would still be here. Me. It was *me*."

I shake my head. Hot tears stinging beyond my eyes. "That's right, you. Don't you see? I choose *you*, Nicholas. Not the prince," I move to him and let my gaze settle on each symbol. The monarchy between us. "You knew, all along, that Finley had been trying to control me?" I look up into his eyes. "You lied." He looks down. "But so did I." Eyes brighter than I'd hoped lift. "I should have told you sooner, I shouldn't have lied about not knowing who the hidden heir was this whole time. I wanted to know the truth as much as you did, I wasn't even sure I believed Finley at first, but I would never have written a lie, Nicholas. Never."

Finley told me that morning, before the river, the mourning bells...so much has changed since the days ago he told me that somehow, I had to get close to the prince, because there was a story to chase. He'd been brazen enough to tell me he was the rightful heir to the throne, without proving to me *how*. Hateful man.

Finley deceived both of us, threatening us with more lies to keep us cowering. He just didn't count on his lies leaking the truth when we compared them.

Unintentional state secret indeed. It wasn't about succession, for us, it was about the parents we lost.

"I found it all, Nicholas. All the evidence Finley had of his legitimacy I found late yesterday. He may have the blood of kings, but he doesn't deserve it." My hands fist at the full extent of what I found. "I burnt the documents that proved royal legitimacy—his birth certificate and an uncensored hospital record and letters between Finley's mother and your grandfather—I burnt it all."

A speck of light as Nicholas raises an eyebrow at my admission. I wave his question off; he doesn't need to know how I came across the code to my publisher's safe through a hidden cipher in Father's journal. I figured it wasn't illegal breaking-in if I knew how to unlock it.

I continue, "I left his claims to the throne in cinders and came here to you instead."

His eyes don't even widen his perception is so instant. Then his gaze narrows. "You protected me instead?"

I can barely nod. It wasn't for him, at first. It was for my father and my mother. I don't know how or when it changed, but somewhere between the bells of time, something shifted. I think of the note Finley left the prince on the last day of mourning. How he tried to use me to expose the Garcon secret without thinking I would find out who he truly was, thinking he could keep me under his thumb, that I would remain unaware that he was the one person I would fight against.

Because he's evil, he never counted on love.

Because he's evil, he never counted on Nicholas telling me the truth or me, accepting it.

The journal was the key, because we shared it. If I hadn't known about my father's words, or his saving the young princes, I would never have thought to look for proof of someone more important than a hidden heir. That there was a crime worse than treason.

I found the secret that killed my father, and it wasn't just Finley being heir...it was Finley ignoring Father's repeated worries about the canal, and Finley, quashing the discussion of experts who may have been able to fix the dikes before the unseasonal rainfall the year of the Yorkson Tragedy. How he threatened them to silence so that no one ever knew, I didn't want to know.

My worries also confirmed that Finley had a deeper intent for sending me to write this story. A deep cruelty that was personal. And yet, it's worse, for Finley didn't think I'd find out he was responsible for my father's death—I assume Finley was the one who somehow made it look like suicide. But worst of all, Finley had wanted me to do his dirty work now to discredit the royal family, all while watching my pathetic self unknowingly treading through a painful past I was intricately tied to.

But now, I know. And I won't leave this story alone until I face Finley.

"It's yours," Nicholas says, soft in the cavern of decision. "You hold my fate in your hands. You must reveal that I'm a fraud, that my ancestors lied to get me here. What has this cost you?"

I shake my head. I would've spent my life protecting him. "We both already paid the price, didn't we? And now, only you decide what to do with this story, with this truth." I don't know what Nicholas will do, now that he knows the challenge to his throne is legitimate.

But if I understood why he was weeping before I arrived, it's because he's already decided his fate.

"It had to be you," Nicholas says in a voice I've come to love, filled with sorrow I don't want to hear. "You kept me alive, I think. It was less lonely, knowing you were somewhere out there, feeling the same way I was. No one else could have understood. But you *existed* and for so long, that was enough." It's like the poem between us, words branded on our surviving souls, words bringing us together. Words that might someday answer why we live when others do not. "You are the reason my feet are planted—why I stayed in this world." His hand rests on my shoulder, holding me to the ground.

This is it, our connection. "Why are we like this?" I whisper brokenly. "Would it not have been better for us to have been taken with them, swept into the waters of memory instead of this living wasteland? Grief and struggle and for what?" I sniff in pain, but before I can wipe its tracks he reaches for my face.

"Don't cry." Strong hands frame my face so I cannot look away. "I'll do anything you want, say anything you want, be anything—"

I slap at his wrists, halfhearted and despairing that the only touch he gives is comfort, because I want to hold onto this bitterness. No one is left alive who can take it from me. But just because he's closest to the reason to blame doesn't make him deserve it.

"Please, don't," I rasp. "I just need a second." I take two steps away.

Stricken. Had I physically attacked, it might have hurt him less.

Nicholas points to the door with a jingle of heavy uniform finery. "I don't have a second. I must go out there and tell the world the lies this family's been living under. Or not. You already had time to live with your lies."

"Wasn't it all a lie?" Between us and the vestry, I finally speak my nearest fear. "And it wasn't all a lie, for my part—I didn't tell you everything about the situation to keep your position safe." I sniff as he backs away, pulling a folded paper from his pocket. "Just because I didn't admit to my feelings for you doesn't mean I was lying to you."

He holds today's article between us. The picture from our kiss yesterday and the column, so small. Stories, words, letters all speaking of the past between us, flowing like a river.

He shakes his head and crosses back to me, the tap-sound of every step he takes an apology. "Do you see this photo? It captured something."

A moment of love. That's how it looks. I want to stay there—live there—forever. If only my heart could speak.

His focus is intense. "How can a picture tell a story—?"

—*and a story tell a picture?* It tries, my heart. But I still can't speak. In books they say eyes say something. I hope to heaven the quaking inside is finally showing up as truth to him.

He nods, once. A gentle lowering of his chin, a letting go. "This was true, this picture, this story. It wasn't wrong, we were, Penelope, we were. Before, then, but not now." He takes another step closer. "I don't want to live in that hell anymore, beneath the lies." Decision settles in deep eyes. Solid, sure, and like trees in a wood, the resolve has grown into something wilder than a forest. "I'll do whatever it takes to leave it all behind." He touches each teardrop-star on his collar, methodical, like they're about to fall. "You're the only star I need anymore."

I'm drawn to the closeness of the almost-king. "I wish you didn't have to do this." I stare at the insignia on his shoulders, knowing deep inside what he's decided to do.

Both his hands take mine. My fingers brush cool medals that clink lightly, as he covers his heart with our clasped grasp. "Every beat of my heart is for you. I'm yours." *It cannot be,* says one voice. *It might be,* says a stronger one. If my heart explodes with happiness, the yearned-for hope so near, will it keep beating? "It's loud, isn't it? What we hear in silence?" He leans down, his forehead on mine. I close my eyes, his voice brushing over me. Warm, when the world seems cold. "We can't stay in here forever."

I nod. I can't speak for this one endless moment. We both know what he has to do.

Then I whisper, "I'm always on your side even when I cannot be beside you." Fighting for him means writing for him. I can't live his story, but I'll tell it—whatever happens tonight. I push him away. "You have somewhere you need to be."

He nods, eyes capturing my soul. "It feels like I've waited an eternity for a stolen second I can't even keep." His lips brush my temple, his hand grazes my neck. His eyes run over me before he walks away. "You're beautiful."

I can't explain how I feel so sad, in the long, lonely minutes that follow. The only star a teardrop twinkling inside my heart. *Tick-tock. Tick—*

I can hear it. The calls of a herald, the ringing of the bells directly above, as it starts to snow.

The false prince, now a king.

I step across the chill of echoing,
cold stone reflecting my dress's

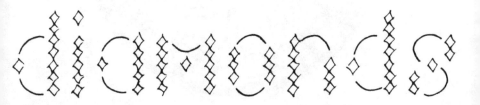

walking across the heavens for him.
I would cross all the stars of the
universe for him.

Two hours earlier...

Gloria Beaumont posing for The Loirehall Times society pages.

THE CORONATION BELL

December 21ˢᵗ, twilight and streetlight, and before the blue dress

Winter light—my favorite starlight—and the dreary winter filtered through the second story windows. Better reached by a hint of warmth, the trying angle of light never gave up, not even on the darkest day of the year.

Blissfully unaware of coming darkness, the sun set between clouds leaving a space for the star leaving the horizon. One star setting so others have their time to shine.

Too quickly, the light left.

Oppression arrived in the form of layered brocade silk and bruised midnight hues of blueish black.

I walked out to meet Madame Vera Eugenie Beaumont, who was flanked by a swinging black train and her daughters. Gloria, in a navy raw silk gown and black accessories, refined, ever trying to rise above her status. And Melody, a shimmery sky-hydrangea-blue dress holding her petite frame but clashing against the pallor of her skin.

It smelt like snow.

My step-aunt stepped forward. I flinched as she flicked off the shoulder of my velvet cape.

"Where did you get this?" Vera asked, tugging the pastel pink neckline of my dress. I didn't answer and she rubbed the luxurious fabric between her fingers. "That hobbyist historian should keep her business with antique books instead of stepping into the present where she doesn't belong. Next thing you know she'll buy the paper."

She brazenly mocked the first woman to rise to an editorial role at any of the publications in Loirehall, but she wasn't wrong about Azalea wanting to buy the newspaper, so I didn't respond.

"I have a message for you," Vera said mildly, tapping her chin, her fingernails long and narrow. She should have worn gloves. "He came by earlier, Finley. Awful man." I didn't disagree. "Isn't he your publisher?"

I managed a nod.

"He said to remind you of your story." I thought of the documents I discovered late last night. I had so much more than the story I planned for. Her smile pierced the knot in my stomach. "Petty nonsense and a waste of time, your writing, storytelling and words worth nothing. Just like your father. Look where that got him." Then she handed me a spare piece of ripped paper.

I read the note by the light of the lamppost. Tomorrow's column, drafted in Finley's voice and choppy ink, with space for me to fill in the rest. He wanted me to write the wrong story.

I *could* write it. It could be dramatic story, at least, with beautiful words. Before I met Nicholas, I was prepared to try anything—to do anything—to write my way into the publishing world. I had taken Finley's claims and thought I could simply prove them. Who cared if Finley was an heir—what had the Garcons ever done but cause me pain? Not that I believed Finley had more than forged documents, which I was also prepared to use to disprove his claims if it came to it. That was my plan until I compared what I found late last night to the details on the portraits in the stuffy hallway of heads in the palace.

Then I knew. Finley's birth certificate, which I obtained, among other documents, from his safe in his office at the publishing house late last night. His middle name the same as Nicholas' father's, a family name: Augustus Leopold Irwin III. His brother, Phillipe Leopold Irwin II Garcon, Duke of Carlingsen, The sixth King of Loirehall. The last king of Loirehall, until tonight, when Nicholas would become King.

No one knew, yet.

I crinkled Finley's page of half-written article in my fist. I could write it all into a tragic story, or at least, a cautionary guide for investors. Anything. I wanted to write my way out of my childhood house and my pain, but this story only kept driving me back to the beginning.

Like fate. Because the prince returned and found me and now, we were waiting for the most important bells.

I hadn't noticed Vera's hazel eyes hardened. I didn't have time to flinch before she struck.

I wished to leave. Like I used to wish, over and over. A wish for every moment I shared in that house with her, my evil step-aunt who raised her voice often and her hands sometimes. Her unkindness a cruelty with small things—a ripped paper, a stubborn stain, how she picked her way into the details of my small, daily life just to torment me.

A wish for every tear of my dress as she yanked and tore my sleeves.

Dear God, I thought I prayed, in the midst of Vera's chaos. Her anger, her pain. I wished and wished and wished for a different ending, because I couldn't have a different story.

Through the evening dark, a snowflake fell in front of us.

It melted as it landed, for the world was not quite ready for winter. Wrenley Square was already abandoned by people who were staying out of the cold, joyfully preparing for the Coronation Ball.

I shivered, my left sleeve gone, the strap ripped off. There was no room left for revenge. Instead of her sharp nails breaking me, she had only torn her invisible truth into the scraps left of my dress.

She was tormented, but I could no longer glory in it, so it made me sad. I thought my bitterness protected me, but freedom felt much nicer. And like my dress was no longer beautiful, I was no longer hers. I never had been.

Somehow, I ended up on my knees. Vera whipped around me, yanking off one of my shoes as my palms scraped on frozen cobblestones. Finley's crumpled note fell into a nearby storm drain as Vera ranted about Father's journal and called me unrepeatable words because I stole it.

I'll never forget the sound of my shoe shattering.

"I've never seen such a useless thing. You shan't use it or go to the Coronation Ball to further whatever this fake relationship is you've corrupted the prince with," Vera seethed, avoiding all she'd broken and walking away into the night.

Melody came around and wrapped her scarf around me. "I'm so sorry. We should have done something."

I shook my head. No, they couldn't.

The glass slipper was broken. Sparkles, a pile of wishes. Not one, but uncountably many. There had never been anything so beautiful. I reached for it—

Gloria's voice was strained. "Don't touch, the glass is sharp." She'd done nothing while Vera tore me apart, I'd nearly forgotten she was there.

Another voice interceded. "It won't cut you; it was tempered glass. See how strong it is?" Azalea came out of her bookshop and all us girls looked up at her, which seemed impossible for she was shorter than us. "Even when you try and break it, it simply shatters into a million pieces and becomes the most gorgeous glitter you've ever seen."

"I like that." Melody swiped a tear.

Gloria stood up, now above me, forlorn. "Maybe in another life we might've been better to each other." She looked away.

She was not all darkness, she'd missed out—such a lightless life. I was not sorry Melody and I had found friendship. I hoped some-day Gloria would see evil for what it truly was. Like we shared a sad past, perhaps someday we could share a future. Even if that someday took forever, I had to believe in it.

"This is our life. Our only life." I let my emotions drill into her. I needed her to believe me. I wanted her to. The final pages weren't written yet, there could be a better ending. "Someday you need to decide to live it well."

She stayed silent, then walked away in the direction her wicked mother went.

Broken—my heart, my dress. Shivering, I tucked my knees into my chest. I couldn't believe this, yet I could. I also just felt sad.

"For once in my life, I was going to be on time." I sniffed. Snow was in the air. We just couldn't see it yet.

"Chin up." Azalea stood above me, wisps of her hair weightless in winter breezes. "What do you see in the sky?"

"In space, there is no up." Pettily, I looked at the ground, avoiding the clouds of night. "I see shapes. Scary shadows. Stories in stars."

Azalea spoke kindly. "Some people in this life are meant to be. A cluster of stars, gravity keeping us together." There was a smile in Azalea's voice as Melody helped me up. "The stars aren't the only ones moving, we are. It isn't over. You have a whole life left to fill with so much gratitude, and it will be so long that no one will remember you were anything different. That bitter? That taste on your tongue that hurts your spirit? Let it lie," she patted my head as tears streamed down my face, "let it lie."

"And tonight?" I wondered.

"Why, it's a ball! The ball of a generation! It will be beautiful." She led us out of the dark of night into the toasty bookshop, muttering about how *watching over this girl for her father is turning out to be a hasty bit of godmother business,* which made me sob even more.

Ting. Chiming, cheery bell. Welcoming in flavors of forgotten leather and steeping tea and precious paper.

I asked what I feared. "Why do tales never show the heroine's point of view, when she descends the stairs to a grand ballroom?" The crowd in finery, and she'd never looked so splendid and the prince—her true love, her soul mate—was waiting for her. In my mangled dress, I couldn't imagine living that sort of moment, not anymore, no matter how many whispered wishes. "Why do we only ever see her from a distance?"

THE DREAM DANCE

December 22nd, present time, moments after midnight and the beginning of the Coronation ceremony

I pretend it's spring, for it's snowing. As if for a moment instead, blossoms fall around us and there isn't a hint of a chill in the air.

Finley's taken me from the coronation, from the steps of church. My struggling sounds are overcome by the tolling of the bells I've loved so much.

My dream is too desperate, so I send wishes to the stars. They'll listen, won't they? Even the center of our rock is molten, hot and bubbling and alive. But up here in the open air, it's hard to believe, now that rough arms snatched me and covered my head. *Will someone save me?* Will anyone save us all?

Ding, dong. Ding—

The coronation bells keep ringing as I'm dragged away. I'd meant to hear them alone—I couldn't watch the ceremony or bear to hear the soft singing before the moment in the coronation—so like a wedding—where Nicholas should've remained motionless as the words *do you have any reason to forgo the burden of this crown?* were spoken over him.

I won't know if he stayed silent or broke his peace, because instead, I'd been sitting outside on stone steps as wide as the church soared in spired steeples above me, but just when I noticed a pile of ashes, and smelt the lingering scent of ink and tobacco, a hand had covered my mouth and forced me away.

The coronation. The ball. The solstice. It's all almost over.

The abdication—did I miss it? Did he do it?

None of that matters, because it's all about to begin, again.

Rough hands yank the hood off my head. The leather is wrecked on the corner of the seat I've been gripping as we drive off, leaning as far I can into the car door. Away from the smell of my publisher and his nefarious presence.

His gaze mocks.

I am disgusted. "You are no king," I spit back at his sly expression. He's missing the coronation ceremony too, so he mightn't know what Nicholas planned to do. "The truth will come out one way or another. Not even you can rewrite my story."

Finley sneers at my vehemence. "You'll go in there to that stuffy ball and give yourself one last chance," he says. "You want your column? All your own? Write the story I want." I peel away from his eagerness, his overdue grudge filling the too-small space between us. "I have been denied too long."

Defiance fills me. "I won't give this to you."

Careless arrogance from Augustus Finley, the hidden heir. "I don't believe you."

"You don't have to," I shoot back.

It never made sense, before. But I look at Finley now and know with all my heart: Father's sacrifice was not in vain. He'd been afraid, I think, of Finley, and it turned out he was right. He must have known how deep the treachery went. But when it truly mattered, Father was brave, and he was strong, strong for Nicholas and Pierre.

And because of his bravery that day, I now have someone to fight for. *Nicholas*, I wish on the stars watching beyond the window. I'll speak for him and fight for him with my every breath. With whatever I have left.

No more past haunting the present. No more darkness.

I may have started this story with the intention of only helping myself, but now, I have so much more to say.

Something strong like steel climbs up my neck. "Let me go."

"Tell the right story," Finley threatens, telling the driver to stop.

I step from the car into welcoming winter air. Beautiful, clear and clean and true.

Apparently, he's got somewhere else to be, as he shouts at his driver to get moving.

But his menace follows me as he calls out the window, leaving me on the road outside Château Fleur. "There's still time, but not much. Write it well."

December 22nd*, after midnight, in the Stardrop Ballroom*
I walk into the ball, afraid.

It's the first dance. Light sparkles on the floor from the ceiling—inside-stars. The steps down are steep.

The ball, so beautiful, it's all before me and I don't want to fall.

My prince—my king. *There he is.* He looks alone in the sparkling world below.

This is the point of view I'd wondered about: the descent into a grand ballroom, magnificent and desperate, like Azalea said. A cube of chandeliers hovers above the square space, the ceiling covered with cherubs in gold and white, glowing above, as people glow below. Velvet and fur finery, silk and jewels reflecting a prism of colors worthy of the palace. Worthy of a coronation.

How could I have ever thought I'd be worthy of a king?

I had looked in a mirror, before I turned the corner into this falling I can no longer avoid. I look splendid, the dress unmarred, unwrinkled, the flush on my skin appealing, the fear seeping out and new feelings overtaking it. Love—

Love.

Love.

Love.

Nicholas turns, walking through the dancers. Lean and regal, his bearing and uniform.

Distance.

His name floats on my breath, but he can't hear me from across the ornate ballroom. The opulent ceiling is several stories high, there are three tiers of scattered balconies, and it's all indescribable elegance and the scent of candle smoke. Voices, muted and muffled, sharing scandal amid bustling finery.

It's the moment I wanted described, and the emotion propelling me forward is so far apart from the situation, so unaligned with the threat following me here, that Azalea's words still ring true. Who can write such an ocean? *Can I cross it?*

But then, Nicholas inclines his head from afar, as if he hears me calling him. As if he's been waiting for me.

Across shadows from light strewn across the checkboard ballroom floor, he comes for me. People bow, ladies curtsey, as a path opens easily before his every step along the dove-gray and winter-white star designed as the starlit center of the ballroom floor. Moving across it, there's a wave of murmured whispers, likely about the earthshaking evening's events. The ball continues, abuzz with the political ramifications of his unexpected choice, but I ignore the sound. All I want to hear is his voice.

He catches my eyes from below one side of a curving staircase, but he doesn't wait, he runs up to the stair below me.

I can't move.

Ever so gently, he extends his hand to my hair, trapping a lock between deft fingers. "Was it snowing outside?" he asks. "What took you so long?" He smiles into my eyes, finally at peace. *He let it go*, I realize with surety, *he abdicated*. It wouldn't be real until he told me, but the sparks in the air tell the story I missed when Finley took me. "You came. Why did you come? Please tell me—"

"To be with you," I answer, for this no other reason, except perhaps, the other one. To leave the world behind. But that's not a real answer, not when he's standing in front of me and looks like he wishes he could kiss me.

"There's a whole story in there," he wipes my tear. I sniff and smile. It's a whole book. Keen eyes examine my face and there's a deep sound at the back of his throat. "A teardrop shaped story. Sounds sad."

I nod, then shake my head. "These are a little happy. Like a happy ending that makes you cry."

"Oh, that's even worse."

"It's good to be sad something happy is over." I breathe deeply, ribs filling the stiff cage of my sparkling blue dress. Nostalgia isn't wrong. "But it's also okay to be glad something sad is ending."

He takes both my hands, leading me, descending the last stairs. "Which is it?"

Music settles around us, calm in a motion. "I'm not sure yet," I reply, achingly hopeful. "You'll have to tell me."

I close my eyes and make a wish. I open my eyes as my very own Prince Charming swings me into his arms.

A waltz. A parade of colors dancing around us. Gloria passes by in a swirl of painfully perfect form, her escort tall and enamored with her. She seems enthralled, but then she catches my gaze, and her eyes widen as she looks warily to her mother. I spin by Vera in the crowd, the starfire bursting from her rhinestone choker defying her dark expression, beady eyes following my happy turning.

Like freezing winter floats, men in dark-hued tails and white bowties and waistcoats spin ladies in myriad dresses, snowflakes in hues of amber, jade, and pearl.

We dance, and like every King and Queen, it ends.

It was a dream, an impossible dream.

When Nicholas drops my hands and bows, I forgo the curtsey and run for an outer balcony. I find a small one with concrete railings designed like swirls on stone, stars welcoming me as freezing air stings my cheeks.

I want to pretend we're alone in a palace all our own, and that the world isn't about to find out everything and everything will change.

Footsteps rushing, now stopping.

Nicholas found me. "Pens." His voice is marvelous and all I'll ever want.

"No." I sigh in happiness. He could always catch me.

He laughs, low and relaxed. "Say no all you want." His arms encircle me from behind. "I don't know why I ever let you run away." A hint of happiness coats his voice too. Relief, to finally be past the ceremony.

Ending is its own kind of relief.

Warmth covers my shoulders; my goose-bumped arms relax beneath an ivory faux fur.

"Azalea passed me on the way out, saying you'd need this," he says, holding me in front of him, his voice in my ear. "I'll listen to whatever you say, all I want is to hear you speak. Just never tell me to leave, please. I can't."

I try to turn. He holds me still. I feel his hair against my cheek. I sigh at his touch, his hands pressing the coat around me.

Our agreement to have a fake relationship meant more. So much more. I don't know what is real anymore. But I'm afraid to believe what's being crushed between us might be real.

It's starting to snow.

Cold air catches my breath. I berate myself for not fighting the joyous possibilities that could break my heart, for leaning into his arms. His chest is solid behind me.

"You can't do what?" I ask, needing to know he's choosing me like I've chosen him. "Am I too much? I don't believe—I don't know how to believe, after the way we kept the truth from each other," I can't speak through my confusion and the cold, my heart beating erratically as I try again, "I don't know how to believe in us."

"You should believe *me*. After all this, believe me. Please." He turns me to face him. So close, his eyes dark embers of a forest and his jaw set. "I have never lied about you. Every word I've said about my feelings for you are true. I have not changed. I can't do this," his eyes flick between our bodies, "because it's fake. I can't do this, because it isn't real." My eyes fill at his declaration. "I can't say anything to you anymore that isn't true, and the only true thing left—the only thing I have left after what I've done—is that I love you. I love you, deeply. With all my heart." His voice catches on cold air, his throat working, saying the words he said before. "All my heart."

I blink at teardrops embroidered in impossible gold on his collar, tracing his angled features to his lips. *I love him.* There's a jar inside me filled with golden wonder and if I open it, the world will see it sparkle. I won't be able to clean it up, the glitter will fill the air and everywhere—

He kisses me. I feel my foot leave the ground, leaning into him and tasting something sweet on his mouth, scorched by the heat of his skin pressed into mine and trying to fly away into this moment and make it last forever.

He draws back, holding me in his eyes—red rimmed eyes, filling with tears. He blinks twice, rapidly, then a single tear slips out the corner of his eye. I truly accept what I'd been hearing, what the murmurs around us meant, whispers of what I'd refused to believe since I arrived at the ball.

My heart. "I wanted you to be King," I say on a breath, knowing what he's given up. "I wanted you to be my king."

His hands don't release me, and he doesn't deny it. "I am no king if I am not first yours."

I squeeze his hands, amazed at how he's able to let it all go. "One day?"

"It's a formality." He smiles, sad, turning to survey the gardens. Vast palace lights are soon lost in the expanse of midnight darkness in the encroaching forest nearby, beneath softly falling snow. "King for a day, and then the monarchy is no more," he whispers.

Smiling as he turns to me, I run my fingers along his hair, fixing it. It's softer than I expected, so I leave my hand reaching up and resting on his head. Glowing lights his features as his eyes study my face, then rise to the parapets and the palace soaring above us. Glowing, like people whose brightness can't help but shine in the dark of the world.

In a flash, urgent fingers wrap around my wrist. Bringing my hand away from him not to push me away, but to protect me. He pulls me beside him, stepping slightly forward.

Declan. No tie. Open collar, overlarge overcoat. He leans to the side to hand me a folded paper.

I open it, glad for Nicholas' silent protection. I read, then glance fearfully into Declan's eyes. He is here for Finley. Devious, but also afraid.

Declan crows at Nicholas. "Any comment for the papers tomorrow about your abdication? Over five hundred years and the monarchy has breathed its last? Using it for the first time in the royal family's long history took guts, but I always thought that protocol was a joke," he jeers.

Nicholas answers in a steady, quiet voice, but I can't comprehend because of the words I'm re-reading.

"Nicholas," my voice gives out. My dear Prince, no longer prince, only a one-day king. The boy I wanted to love, my whole life. Just him. But I can't breathe. "I almost got my wish." I wished my whole life to know him and now I have to leave him.

Nicholas had given in to a lie, but I had given in to the silence. Now that he's defied the lie, I can no longer be silent. We might resist the fear, finally, when we tell the truth, together.

If we get a chance, after this.

Sterling hovers near the doorway, joining us in the cold. Watching as Declan smugly leaves, ever watchful in a jacket with sharp tails, a sun-radiant waistcoat and royal blue top hat with accents to match. But his expression? It matches the caving in of my heart.

It is everything impossible—grief and sadness. I can't stop the ache in my lungs and my hair flows behind me as I rush down the stairs into the gardens and the paths beyond. I know where in the woods we need to go.

"Why are you—" Nicholas' voice drops. I know he'll follow. He won't let me face this alone. He races after me. "Wait," he calls again, he calls for me.

December 22ⁿᵈ, a rush of steps later

In the depths of the forest, there's no light from stars too high in the trees.

We race to the place it all started. False, fake light. Not stars, but streetlamps lining the canal.

"Your Majesty," Finley's tobacco-roughed voice mocks. "It's ironic, don't you think? You could see over four thousand stars if we weren't surrounded by streetlamps. This is no dark sky, there is too much created, false light crowding out the night. Fake, like you."

My slippers are soaked. Feet freezing, heart frozen in terror. Nicholas precedes me, holding a hand out to me as I slow down, sheltering me with his body.

"No amount of royal blood would've made you worthy of the crown," Nicholas replies, steadfast.

I wish I didn't know why we were out here, but it's the one place in the world Finley would bring us to remind us of the pain he inflicted on our families, the pain he can still inflict.

I won't let him.

Water of the Valais River streams nearby, where both our parents died. Where *he* killed them, where he let the river take them and the car he'd sabotaged claim them.

Part of me grieves to have found the whole truth last night. But Azalea once told me that stars make their own light and that our ability to see them isn't just about their brightness, but the distance to us.

So, I glance around the dark, looking for light. Finley doesn't want the crown to cease, he wants to be king. What will he use to force it? How far will he go? He wasn't at the coronation ceremony when Nicholas abdicated. Does he even know his chance is already gone?

It's become fearfully quiet.

Nicholas challenges him. "You miscalculated." Resolve hardens his tone, his lips tight. Nicholas angry is something I've never imagined. "You threatened my brother, all these years. This anonymous pecking at the palace window, your yearly missives bland and tasteless. You held his life over my head, this invisible specter, and you expected me to be no better than a puppet on a string when I became King." Nicholas holds my hand in a tight grip, but he's shaking, but not I suspect, from the cold, so much as the details I just relayed to him while running here. Nicholas continues in a strong voice. "I won't let you; do you understand? I won't let you become King."

My heart brims over. Nicholas has never looked more like a King, and it's sad, because Loirehall has already lost her king.

Peace floods me. However this unfolds, it hasn't happened how I expected it to. When Finley first approached me in the alley with my one chance at the column, I thought that was the only chance I would ever get. A lifetime of unanswered wishes and I thought I could take one by force.

I was wrong.

Wrong to doubt my father when I found his journal.

Wrong to doubt Nicholas, when he said he'd let it all go—the monarchy, the throne—for the sake of his family, for memory, for honor. For the *future*. Things a villain like Finley could never understand.

Wrong to doubt myself, as if I wasn't meant to be here in this moment, to bear witness to the end of one thing and the beginning of another.

"Liar," Nicholas says, no longer deceived by Finley. "The world has changed, and you're frozen in another time. This is all you've ever wanted but the throne is already out of reach for both of us, it's over."

"I am the rightful king! Not you, not your ridiculous regent uncle. I have waited so long—"

"It doesn't matter." Nicholas says, confident, his hand holding mine. "The world will hear what she has to say. All of it."

"The world will judge you and your family as false."

"Let them, let them judge me now that I know the truth! Now that I've acted on it. Let them listen." Nicholas holds tighter to me, and I don't doubt it was the right thing to tell him what *else* I'd found out about Finley in his sordid safe. About what documents I *didn't* burn to a cinder. "And you miscalculated her. How cruel you were, sending her into the history that had broken her heart. But you underestimated her. You underestimate the power truth has. Penelope will tell the world and you can pay for your sins publicly, the rest of your life for the life of our Fathers, of our Mothers. You *knew* the dikes wouldn't hold if the waters rose on the river. You knew people would get hurt, and you made sure my parents were in that car that day—you will pay!"

Snowflakes disappear into the calm river as Finley considers, pride making him stumble even at the last.

"I am, after all, not the rightful king," Nicholas says, "but I won't let you take the throne. It's already gone."

It's all in the past, except for these two men.

Finley jerks a chin at me. "Your father's last word was your name. His precious daughter— sickening. Over and over, when I pointed this at him." Finley tips his wrist, revealing a pistol and pointing it at two figures roped to a tree.

A cry escapes my lips. Committed suicide in his office—that's what the papers said about my father. I *knew* it wasn't the truth, before I found Father's journal and his claims about Finley inside it. Now, there's nothing in the world I want more than to have all this end.

But I never knew telling the whole truth would bring *them* into it.

THE LOIREHALL TIMES

DECEMBER 22ND

SPECIAL MIDNIGHT EDITION: ABDICATION OVER-SHADOWED BY ANSWER TO THE MYSTERY OF THE MURDER OF THE KING AND LADY GARCON

Article and photo by Declan Hayes

REVELATIONS AT THE CORONATION BALL REGARD-ING THE ABDICATION OF THE CROWN PRINCE WERE SWIRLING LIKE THE SNOW THAT CARPETED LOIRE-HALL.

Photo: Prince Nicholas Garcon at the Coronation Ceremony, for-mally refusing the crown and scepter

After a shocking refusal to take the scepter and the throne of the Kingdom of Loirehall, Nicholas Garcon briefly attended the Coronation Ball before disappearing. Witnesses say he followed the young lady previously mentioned in this paper into the woods. One comment was given by Azalea Pumpkin, editor at large for the *Times* and member of the royal court, regarding what she overheard. She claims answers to the mystery of the Yorkson Tragedy and the deaths of the Garcon couple will be forthcoming.

The question remains: Why did the King abdicate? Why did he give up the throne? Was it related to the rumored hidden heir?

The only comment given in regard to the abdication was by Councilor Figgleston—before dramatic events disrupted the ball—who said that there were questions of royal succession but that the Garcon family was determined to move forward with constitutional changes, which included Nicholas Garcon's decision to abdicate in order to remove the monarchy to the place it deserves in history, which was the next logical step in Loirehall's future.

Figgleston noted that in such cases, the state would continue with the modernization process regardless of the family member presiding over it, as the legal teams from neighboring governments had already begun talks with the Duchy's regional council. At the time of printing, it is still assumed that the King—who remains so only for twenty-four hours from the ceremony, due to the irreversible Abdication Clause his actions invoked—will be the individual at the head of the monarchy for the time that remains, and will continue in a diplomatic, advisory role in the future.

But later, the King was seen at the palace, calling for a doctor and his guards, claiming he'd caught the murderer of his parents.

Can it be that same person is the hidden heir? Rumors of the heir's identity and the captain's critical condition were unconfirmed at the time this went to press, after midnight.

THE SEARCH BELL

December 22nd, too long after midnight

I will live an entire lifetime worth the remembering of this moment.

So many stars. So much darkness.

A tick. Not of a clock, but of breaking sticks beneath our feet in the forest beneath Polaris.

And a click. Not of a camera, but of a pistol safety undone.

There is nothing left, and there is everything. The two people Nicholas and I care most about in the world held at gunpoint by a desperate man, ropes strapping them to a tree and gags over their mouths.

"Such convenience." Finley sneers. "I found them together on a midnight stroll." The weapon waves restlessly toward Melody and Max. "Did you know about this? It's a whole other story, though not worth telling."

Fear permeates the air.

"Stay back." Nicholas shoves me behind him, though I wish I could run to Melody. "He won't shoot." His voice is cool, colder than forested, frosted air. Cold air rushes too quickly in my lungs and I cough, not sure I agree—Finley killed my father. Nicholas nods to our friends. "Let them go, Augustus."

"Her father was nosy too, getting himself tangled up in the same desperate need to know." Finley bores of the past, shifting the gun, his motions agitated.

Nicholas stands his ground. "Your time has passed. It's already over. The throne would never have endured another decade and now, it will never suffer a murderer. You and I are no family. I mean what I said, Augustus, it's gone. The throne is no more," Nicholas' voice resounds in the dark woods. "I abdicated. I invoked the Abdication Clause and in twenty-four hours there will be no more crown to be had."

Finley stills, stunned. He knows enacting abdication is irreversible and dissolves the monarchy—he's ruthless but smart. "How could you? How can you give it up?"

"Eventually, even a constitutional monarchy fades," Nicholas says, confidence radiating from his choice, and the wisdom in it. "It all fades with time. There is no more crown for Loirehall; whatever was left of the old kingdom is gone. It cannot be undone."

Rage pauses the motion of air around Finley. "Then you won't need him." He raises the gun at Max.

In a flash it happens—the shot, the shout, the shudder of Max's body as he buckles, constrained by the ropes. Blood grows on his chest like an exploding star through the white of his dress uniform.

It's Melody's cry that lingers.

Nicholas races for Finley and I undo the ties strapping our friends to the tree trunk. As soon as their bonds are loose, the captain falls to his knees, then falls forward. I gently roll Max, his face snow-caked and sore.

"Max," Melody sobs.

In the distance echo deeper voices and a scuffle. I throw my body over my friends as another gunshot rings out through the air.

Nicholas stands, shocked, the gun smoking in a dead Finley's hand as he topples back into the river.

"Go," I call to Nicholas. "Max needs you! It's the only way to get help. They won't listen to me, but they'll listen to you. You're still the king!" He obeys my entreaties and sprints away.

Our world is too loud.

And it isn't just the noise or the cars or the hum of unidentifiable electricity. It's the sound of hurry. The shout of hustle. The cry of trying and the whimper of failing. But now, this quiet, snowfall world seems wrong too. This dying is subtle. Humble, on the darkest night of the year. I'm witness to a softer ending.

If only the sound of joy and peace and love were more common, then the world would be a gentler place.

This world of snowfall and endings is so very quiet. I listen carefully and remain silent, learning, like the world, how to be better.

Melody frees herself from the scratchy remains of her ropes.

"Please don't cry," Max whispers. I hold my hand hard against his blood-drenched chest, pressing against the fatal wound. Melody holds his head as he speaks only for her. "I always dreamed of someone like you."

"I already got my wish," she replies.

"Melody, what if this is it?"

"This isn't the end, my dear Max," she says sweetly. I wonder at the strength in her sweet voice. "I'll find you in eternity. I'll find you somewhere peaceful and warm and if you get there before me, save me a spot at the table. I'm coming. I'll be coming."

A serene smile, just for her. "I'll be waiting."

There's something between them I may never understand. My silence is the only good thing here.

"White is my favorite color," he says to her.

I swallow a sob as she smiles back at him, radiant. I would've thought white wasn't a color, and I may never change my mind, because blood covers my hands and the white uniform is soiled in a way I will never forget.

Max's forehead creases as he struggles to speak. "All that possibility, in white, in the unknown. You can create anything you want to, if you just start with—" he cringes back and closes his eyes, pain marring his features.

Her head shakes. "All will be shadow," she whispers as he loses consciousness. A grayish pallor falls across his skin, beneath the false streetlamp light, dim. "If you leave, I'll find beauty in the shadow, I promise."

A wind blows through the forest. A breeze lifting the snowflakes before they touch the ground and for a moment, falling is flying.

I lift my eyes, but there is no wish left to make in this moment. This picture isn't filming. There is nothing to capture but shadow. It's pencil, charcoal. Dark on light.

My eyes close to an image. A crown of daisies floats down the river. The little girl and her littler sister losing the royal jewels to the current, chasing and shrieking and filled with tragic delight.

I can't tell if it's the present or the future. Both break my heart. I hear bells. The search bells.

December 22ⁿᵈ, in the aftermath

"The starlight and air made this forest, and it grows by the light of the star." Melody brushes snowflakes from Max's face. "May that star guide you home."

"You were supposed to have the song." I say to her. Max is quiet now. This is the wrong silence, the wrong scene, the wrong story. "It's not the right song."

"Tonight was yours," she says, gracious yet far from me, for it's because of my story *her* love story must end here. "Your future is safe now."

"Melody—" I can't. I wish I could say. How can such grief and loss be articulated, the what if, the what might have been? All that possibility, just gone. "I'm so sorry."

"Why are the most wondrous songs not made of pure joy? Because you wouldn't hear the sweet refrain of the melody without the dark notes beneath." She speaks softly, and to herself it seems, not to me. "They carry it, you see, that difficult harmony. What good is a melody without difficult notes of discord beneath it?"

So many wishes, in life. When mine are so near coming true, hers are lost. It feels like we're so alone, in this dark forest. Starlight shining, somewhere.

"What will you do?" I wonder aloud.

She's only sixteen, but the breaking of her heart seems ancient. "I'll go back to our part of the forest. It's enchanted, you know." Her hands now cover the captain's chest, from which I can't detect motion, his breaths are so shallow. "We even have a cottage on a corner of it."

I want her to have it, forever. "You can keep it," I whisper, hearing gentle sounds from the river. One could almost imagine the soft flakes falling into freezing water, and the sound should be soothing. Instead, it reminds me of all that's being taken, taken away.

"I need to go off the path more often, I think," Melody says, softly. "Someday, someone curious enough might join me. They'd be my favorite."

Why is this happening? Why her? Why now? It isn't fair. All I see is starlight and the dreary winter and another day gone and Max—

"Don't worry," she assures me, "things always change. Toss these frocks," I look down at our dresses ruined by the blood and the snow, "but keep those other dresses Azalea brought in a box, someone might need them someday. They'll hold the heartache and tragedy and after many years, they'll fold those memories into something new, something beautiful." I sniff, but Melody's full of words, waiting while the life of her love seeps into the floor of the forest. "Gloria will marry someday soon, and Mother will get old...but she can never find out about Max. Dark secrets can only grow in shadows, but because this is a good one, I want to keep it for myself."

I simply nod, a teardrop falling onto fresh snow.

A booming voice calls, and it's Sterling. He's standing watch at the edge of the path, near another tragedy. Many footsteps and voices. Guards hover over the river, searching. They drag out Finley's prone body, quietly carrying out orders. Now, Sterling is answering Nicholas as he rushes past, their voices mingling with others.

Nicholas runs to us, and I move out of the way as he kneels beside Max. I settle on the snow-carpeted forest floor. It's calm, *how can it be so calm?*

Nicholas is gentle with his dying companion. Max awakens, blinks at Nicholas, and beneath the smile of his best friend, his soul disappears from our sight.

Sterling gently moves Melody aside as he and Nicholas surround the dead captain.

You would think the aftershocks of an earthquake would be devastating, and they are. But there's something about the dust settling, when the light hits it.

Maybe all our lives are little specks of fairy dust, sparkling through the air, landing back on the earth where we came from when our time is finally done. But while we're able to fly, hopefully we glitter. Hopefully we let the light turn our dusty ashes into beautiful swirls, surrounding all the other passengers on the air trying to find a path in the darkness, reflecting the light to help others on their journey. Making the dust beautiful.

Melody's cries shimmer through the night. The men start back to the palace, but I wait for her. The winter wind of life is trying to break her, but she bends over on her knees. Surrendering.

Where is the wind going? It has no color, no voice but for what is left behind. I think part of Melody is already gone, soaring up on wings that must spend a lifetime remembering. I hope someday her falling becomes flying.

She cries and the world around her holds her gently.

What spirit is this? Is it peace left beyond the fell waste of a storm? I'm just not ready for it yet. Stars and snowflakes, falling falling falling.

Abdication overshadowed
by answer to the mystery
of the murder of King
and Lady Garcon.

The Silent Story

December 25th, just before noon

What story should I tell the world? Should I tell it at all?

Three midnights later I've only written truth.

Abdication was irreversible. Though a true heir, Finley couldn't have taken the crown once the monarchy was dissolved. Nicholas was right, Finley had been unworthy—his life taken by the frenzy of his own blood-stained hands, the ones he'd used to snuff the souls of others.

All those lives, all those secrets like lost wishes tossed into the raging river, no longer forgotten. No longer hidden.

Not even a villain can stay hidden forever. I've written out his story too, at least what I pieced together of it from my father's journal and the documents from Finley's safe. It feels good for my soul to tell it. Letting go of it is making space in my heart for the light instead of holding onto dark.

Melody and Max though, I keep their story a secret, for those who loved them. I know that's what Melody wants—I haven't seen her, but she left a jar with the shards of my broken glass slipper. A reminder that sharp pain fades, and that shattered things can still be beautiful when you shine light on them. Maybe someday, someone will find a use for them other than holding the jar up dreamily to refract perfect and unseeable colors all around.

That's my story.

My mother, lost too soon. My father, his last days after saving the prince at the riverside consumed by fear of the one who'd caused it all and the knowledge of Augustus Finley's real identity.

The late King and Queen and finally Finley gone, finally shown to be responsible for it all. And us, still here. Pierre, his story yet unwritten. Nicholas, strong enough to let go of the past.

And me, living above a bookshop with words beneath me uncountable as the stars.

Then I hear the bells, and it's Christmas Day.

Twisting my wrist, I walk gingerly to look out the window. Sunrise has long passed, and it feels good to stand, to move. Snow isn't falling anymore, it's settled in drifts over the frosted tips of roofs and snowcapped street signs. Some of the snow has already been brushed aside, safe to walk on. The frosted glass is cool on my forehead, yet there's warmth from midday sunlight, melting icicles from above to drip like the second hand of clock.

Tick-tock, tick. Ding, dong. Bells, still ringing in my heart. *Ding—*

A dark figure strides by, his confident bearing pausing in my frame of vision. A long black jacket sweeps around his knees as he looks up. An intricate rose-gold embellishment on the hem and cuff of the regal coat. No longer a king nor a prince. Just alive, his smile—it's the real him. Slightly stiff, though less uncertain, a calm countenance with living fire blazing behind his eyes.

A gust of wind blows snow across my view through the window, and I leave the single frame like a photograph and run to meet my true love. To touch him, to see his face and hear his voice.

In the same second as the cheerful chime of the bells on the door, he's already inside the bookshop and I hardly make it to the stairs; he comes so quickly for me.

Taking the steps two at a time we collide, our hearts beating heavily.

You would think the aftershocks of an earthquake would be devastating, and they are. But there's something about the dust settling, when the light hits it.

I can only close my eyes in delight at the brightness.

If all our lives are sparks through the air, I want to fly well until my time is done. I want to glitter. I want to keep having to blink at the bright, dusty ashes becoming beautiful swirls. Lighting the dark, so we don't feel so alone.

So beautiful.

"It's tomorrow," Nicholas says quietly, holding on.

I don't know why Melody's true love had to die.

"I'll stand with you, mourning on another riverside," I promise. Another funeral, another passing, stardust and a star exploding. "But I need to be beside you, I can't—" I collapse on the stairs, he lowers me gently, standing guard above me.

"Always. Don't be afraid, we'll always be together. And look." He takes something from his inner jacket pocket. In his hand, scattered splotches, dark, upon weighted ivory paper. He waits until I nod that I recognize it and then he returns it to the pocket, tapping his hand over his heart. "I kept some of your forgotten writing, from before. That morning in the journal wasn't the first time you wrote some of those words to the poem. You tried before, until you found the right ones."

I look up at him, forever looking up at his tall form.

"What is the question in your eyes? How do you not know? Penelope," my forever prince says, "it wasn't the words; it was the heart behind them." His voice is a balm, a salve on my wounded soul. "You're like snow, but my dark was daylight and you took your words and the ink blotted it out."

Tears fall like stars. I swipe my mouth, my cheeks. Invisible tracks, invisible pain. How has he seen?

Slow, sure, certain, Nicholas kneels before me. "You can't see love, but it's the most magical thing around us." Strong hands steady me. Our faces are at a level, as he's on the step below me. Gently, he crowds my space, steals my air. "You press too hard." Lean fingers reach my face, gentleness traces tears and covers fears. It heals and his lips smile, soft. "When you write, you press too hard. The ink can't but spill past the page—through it." A quiet laugh, a tremor in his jaw. "You ripped the page, you pressed so hard. But your words have always been—your words *are*—more than what you write on the page. They leave a mark long after you've forgotten them."

I cover my mouth and cry as he continues, "You alone, only you were good for me. You fit into every crevice of my heart that's been too dark. You're shiny and bright and perfect, and your value is priceless." Nicholas and his memory, his words the exact opposite of Declan's accusations.

Now, I feel the warmth of his body as Nicholas leans into me. His kisses taste like tears and safety. Over and over. His lips on mine, ever and again. Peace surrounds our sadness, then his arms surround me.

"You worked so hard," he whispers into my hair.

I sigh. "I finished."

He settles beside me on the top stair, his nutshell brogues dripping wet snow from the heels. "I'm so proud of you."

I lean my head against his arm, exhausted. Used up and empty and satisfied, ready to be filled. Like I can finally rest.

"Only for you," I say, my face against his jacket, rich embroidery scratching my forehead. It's like looking at a star. "You're my prince, the king of my heart. Nothing else matters."

"Always," a smile weaves through his voice. "We'll go, someday soon."

"Where?"

"Anywhere."

I pull back to trace his face. "And what will we do there?"

"I'll ask you to marry me." He kisses me again, colors alive behind closed eyes.

When his lips part from mine, he breathes and pulls back enough to plant another kiss against the hollow of my cheek, back to the corner of my mouth and he speaks again, slow and serious. As if I'm the only thing that matters to him in the whole world. "What made you survive?"

I smile against his lips. "You."

"And your writing."

My chest rises with the truth and falls with our silence. The memory of his compassion, so dear since the moment I met him.

His strength, the thought of it keeping me upright these last days, where I penned the most important story of my life.

I lean back to stare into those green eyes. "Thank you for letting me write about more than how it hurt."

"How many books have you left to fill?" His voice fills my veins with warmth, or maybe it's just his breath against my hair as he hugs me.

Unbidden, a silent sob rises, and I choke it back, resting my cheek on his chest. His beating heart, his heart for me. "So many."

It must be my imagination that a bell rings. I must be mistaken, but he pulls me closer. How can we be closer than we are now?

There's a hope I dare not voice though I saw it waiting in his eyes. "Why—" a bell again, but I thought the noon bells were already past. "Did you hear that sound?"

"I've never been afraid to ask anything in my life." For an honest second in time, his eyes shutter as he pulls away from me. His chin dips to his chest, a shaky breath. No longer prince, in this precious moment I treasure. But he trusts me, I can feel it. He's a man with a simple question and there's only one answer I could ever give, in any world, in any time.

I dare to say it.

"Yes." I answer boldly. Sorry for the sorrow that brought us together. Loving his gorgeous forest-filled eyes, his angular face. "Nicholas, look at me." He obeys, claiming my heart more with every second. "Bells are wishes." I whisper. He tilts his head. A spark of hope, a trying smile. "That's how I hear them, every year." I speak to the sparking air, and he must know I'm baring my soul. Looking away from his penetrating gaze to focus on a knob in the wood on the stairs, leaving behind every painful moment that brought together our history. Oh, that my mind could keep this picture. "Each toll must be a wish, because if it isn't—"

"We'll have to keep listening." A tear collects in the corner of his right eye. I touch it gently and he captures my fingers. "No more despair," he vows, a king no longer, but he's greater.

It's a beautiful miracle that such a man would cry for me. How I treasure his still voice, his face. His heart bare before me.

"No more grieving, at least, not today." I focus on the world alive in his eyes, and I've never wanted to protect anything so much in my life. "No more memory of old fear, old pain. No more days we can't overcome together. The sorrow can remain in streaming waters, and we can visit it to keep the happy memories alive."

He huffs a laugh, dark air leaving, light coming in. He leaves one arm around my waist, his right hand swipes his eyes. "How am I the one giving speeches? I'll follow you anywhere."

"I'm serious."

"So am I."

"No more tears." I whisper to him.

"Not today." Heat from his skin reaches across the thin air to caress me. Both his hands tangle in my hair and I breathe him in, sweet clove and forever forests. "It's over now."

"What do you mean? Isn't this the beginning?" I ask, enjoying his smile against the curve of my neck. A bell tolls again and I startle. "What was that? I'm not imagining it, am I?"

A sound hums in his throat. Non-committal, ever so slightly unsure. I feel it rumble through my chest, pressed up against him as I am.

I shift in his arms. It *is* past noon; those aren't the midday bells. "Nicholas, what did you—?"

"Marry me."

I gasp, pushing him away. "You told them to ring the bells *before* I said yes!"

A self-satisfied smirk, flashing teeth and sparking green eyes. I press my lips together at his charm, holding in the greatest smile of my life.

My dear Prince. My King. My lover, my life. Just him.

I breathe. "I got my wish." I wished my whole life to meet him and now I'll never have to leave him. It is everything wondrous, joy and fullness. I release my smile, and my hair flips sharply as I rush down the stairs and out the door, following a snow-strewn path past the river.

Every day, people will disperse, back to their lives and homes and families. All of us joined by memories and hopes and crushed dreams and hidden wishes, mingling together without any space between them like the glorious ringing of bells.

"Why are you—Pens! You're in bare feet," his voice changes, lifts. He races behind me. "I found you once, I'll find you forever, Penelope Beaumont! Wait—after you marry me, you'll have a new name."

He calls again, he calls for me.

All of us joined by
memories and hopes and
crushed dreams and hidden

mingling together without
any space between them
like the glorious ringing of
bells.

One year
later...

THE LOIREHALL TIMES

DECEMBER 25TH

FORMER KING TO BE MARRIED ON SAINT STEPHEN'S DAY

Article by Publisher Azalea Pumpkin and photo by Declan Hayes

ONE YEAR AFTER THE DRAMATIC ABDICATION OF THE GARCON ROYAL FAMILY, TOMORROW THE HEIR TO THE GARCON LINE WILL MARRY THE WOMAN WHO CAPTURED HIS HEART.

Photo: Nicholas Garcon and his betrothed dancing at the Coronation Ball last year

Penelope Beaumont, the soon-to-be-wife of Lord Nicholas Garcon, is taking time off her regular Sunday column for her wedding and honeymoon. After a whirlwind romance last year with the then-Crown Prince, she was instrumental in finding not only the murderer of their parents from the Yorkson Tragedy, but also in bringing to light the misdeeds generations prior that had brought another successor to challenge the throne. By abdicating when he did, Lord Garcon avoided a constitutional crisis and, in the time since, has worked tirelessly with Mayor and Council to ease the transition of our lovely city and region to a more modern governance.

Before the ceremony tomorrow afternoon, there will be a morning service in the cathedral to honor Maximus Cavendish. In remembrance of the events of last year, the late Captain of the Guard will be rewarded posthumously with a meritorious Diamond Star for his bravery. All are welcome, but please arrive before ten o'clock in the morning.

Expect the society pages of this paper to be thicker than usual after what we speculate will be the largest wedding of the year. Grand starcast banners already wave through the streets of Upper and Lower Towne to honor the so-called One-Day King, whom many still support by adding the royal teardrop star to flags draped in windows of homes and shops every winter solstice. But the real question is, will the roads handle the crowds? If you miss a moment, these pages will cover the whole story for you. For now, you'll hear the bells, this Christmas Day. For tomorrow, listen for wedding bells.

Chiming bells on holy days ring

{painted skies, unveiled facing}

Wishes for lost souls sing

{endless, time racing}

Sacred spells, yearning hearts

{black the tie of borrowed hearts, beating}

Loss and love amid the sound

{pain, bracing}

Chiming bells, 'til peace reigns

{old grief anew, past days—erasing}

—"Passing Grief" by Monsieur Beaumont,
annotations by Penelope Beaumont

Forty years later...

HEARTS

A
HEARTBOOKS
NOVEL

BRITTANY EDEN

PROLOGUE

PART ONE: WONDERLAND

"No, I give it up," Alice replied: *"what's the answer?"*
"I haven't the slightest idea," said the Hatter.
—Lewis Carroll
Alice's Adventures in Wonderland

Seven years ago

I wonder what light drew me beyond my window and onto the roof.

Maybe it was the moon, a great light shining hope in the night.

Because maybe, stars weren't enough for a withdrawn girl. But that great night light illuminated my darkness and brought moments of freedom. There, I found someone. I even caught glimpses of myself—my true self—on the moonlit nights.

Mostly though, I think it was the stars that started it.

"What do you think heaven is like?" my friend asked, hidden in the shadows.

I shivered in my nightgown, which clung in the humid late-night air. "You're asking the wrong question."

I drew my knees up against the late summer chill, feeling hints of freedom from the fog crowding my mind, there in midnight darkness under the wide expanse of the heavens.

Beneath innumerable stars, the city slumbered softly while in the forest beyond the townhouse backyards hummed a nightingale, defying the blare of a passing ambulance siren. It was calm on the rooftop where I spent summer nights keeping vigil against sleeplessness. I could deny the past all I wanted, until I slept. I was too afraid to confront my trauma and desperate to protect myself from what might have been reality or may have been delusions. But there was no hiding in the subconscious, and it didn't seem possible for my young mind to process.

Night-terrors are scary.

"And what would that be?" he asked, lounging like he owned the roof of the shed belonging to the townhouse beside mine, which nearly touched the second story roof I sat on.

I bit my lip. "Where is heaven?" I stared at the crescent moon, glad my unnamed companion shared my affinity for secrecy and mystery. "Where can we find it?"

"Would we know it if we saw it?" His words echoed the longing my heart, because all I ever wanted was to see a glimpse of heaven.

Peace, like the settling of night after a long day. Joy, for endings and beginnings. Love.

I took a deep breath of the cooling night air. "Heaven is endless light making clouds glow with gold-rimmed fire over an ageless sea beyond the stars." Leaves rustled on nearby trees. "Heaven is where hills are split by a happy river whose destination is forever."

"You're just describing the sunset," he scoffed. "That's cheating."

"Maybe the sunset is the start of heaven," I huffed, hurt. "Maybe sunsets lead the way there every night, and God keeps sending them to remind us to keep looking."

"You're just obsessed with sunsets because you hate summer at home so much you want it to end." Hurt laced his voice as it nailed at sharp angles the thing inside I tried to cover, but I swallowed my own cutting reply because I couldn't bear to hurt the one person who'd kept me company on this rooftop for each lonely birthday these last hard years.

Was he right? Was my desire to hide wrong? No amount of whimsical questions had led me to reveal my truth to him, no, I hid that memory so deep, it no longer felt real. The past was a dream, and I had relegated it to my nightmares. If it stayed there, it couldn't haunt me during the day.

But part of me wanted more, to be more than that memory had forced me to become, and all my self-preservation never banished the thought. *There is more.* Just like the sunset was a daily reminder to remember, and surely all remembering wasn't monstrous. The sunset, pulling its rays through the clouds and playing its last strains to the sky long after disappearing. Such steadfast resistance to nature, such futility in the face of another tomorrow. And right then on the rooftop, between me and the boy, darkness had already fallen. It all started five summers ago on my seventh birthday, and none of us were the same since.

How could the heart survive?

THE TEA PARTY

Present day, Sunday

STERLING FIGGLESTON PAUSES beside my hovering. I cling to the sketch in my hand, too cowardly to ascend the seven daunting stairs of the gorgeous white paneled, brick-accented townhouse on the Upper Towne street where I used to live.

"Time for the song everyone's been waiting for." My old godfather takes the first step slowly, holding the railing with arthritic fingers, using his umbrella for balance with the other.

I match his pace. First step. Past mismatched pots smelling of green lining the stairs. Second step. Third. Up steps that seem bigger than they should, even though the street seems smaller than my childhood memories.

I pause to look up at the last four steps to an entrance encased in whimsy, and like Eliza Doolittle said—*wouldn't it be loverly?* "I can't sing."

He grips the handrail tightly as he stops on step six. "You don't have to." With a resonant but gentle voice, he is the epitome of gentlemanly and scholarly all wrapped up in a mischievous, elderly package named Sterling Irwinaeus Figgleston. "Your art sings your heart beautifully."

We both look at the leather laptop satchel I'm clutching to my chest, holding the drawing of a heart that might be the key to my future. Sterling had promised me the best way to build my reputation was to be discovered by someone in a select, niche group wishing to be the first of their friends to discover fresh works of art. We've been aiming for an opportunity precisely like the one Madame Penelope Garcon might give us: exposure in a high-profile event filled with the curated type of people who collect obscure statues and love mysterious artists.

Sterling exhales on the last step and pauses again before lifting the door knocker. Instead of a ghoulish face, it's like a star. Or maybe a flower. It's so intricate it's impossible to tell, but it's a tiny bit sad and I instantly adore it.

"Your idea is perfect," he assures me. "Your art is ready—your aunt made sure of that. And this is the next step, you just have to take it. I helped Melody become Briar Rose, and I promised her you would follow in her footsteps. I won't fail, and neither will you."

For all his quirks, Sterling seems intent on rescuing me from my fledgling attempts to make it all on my own. Grateful for the stroke of fate—or simply the stubbornness of my aunt—that ensured her and Sterling be my godparents, my heart fills with happy hope. I desperately need his help if I want to be the artist Auntie thought I could be, and this scheme might be perfect. "Thank you."

He nods, waiting as I ascend the final stair.

Time to embrace a pen name for my pencils that isn't my own. *Briar Rose.* I'm not sure if I'm the right size to fit in the footsteps of my aunt.

"Wipe that ridiculous expression off your face and focus, Elizabeth," Sterling chides, adjusting his perfectly straight bowtie. It's burgundy plaid, which sounds worse than it looks. "I can tell when your thoughts are being overdramatic."

Two enormous terra cotta pots overflowing with palms stand like sentinels at the front doors. Before I can decide if they're good or evil guards, or simply footmen, the door opens with a gratifying flourish of cool air.

"Madame Garcon." Removing his taupe hat, Sterling dips his black, bald head.

The scent of burnt sugar flows from behind the tall, stately woman. Stylishly attired, she's far past middle age, yet moves with the grace of a willow tree on a quiet afternoon. Her silver hair glitters in the sunlight, gliding to just above her shoulders.

She gestures us into her sweet-smelling home. "Welcome." Her voice sings the word *welcome* in a way that makes me absolutely believe her. "How lovely to see you, old friend." She air-kisses one of Sterling's wrinkled cheeks. "It's been a long time."

"Too long," he agrees, taking her hand gently.

Sunshine from a gorgeous midsummer's day in Loirehall makes Madame Garcon's dainty bracelets glimmer pretty prisms against the silk of her slim-fitting shirt.

"I'm sorry for the Beaumont loss." Madame Garcon's crystalline blue eyes are sincere, laugh-lined and gentle. "Melody was always one for unusual requests. Thank you for taking my cake to them. I hope they enjoyed it."

Oh my word, Madame Garcon made the lemon cake for Auntie's funeral?

I cough at the coincidence. Sterling shakes his head at me as Madame leads us inside. Would she welcome me so graciously if she knew who I truly am?

My chin lowers not just in deference to her regal air and history, but with the heavy memories connected with the name *Garcon* that harken me back to a time I'd rather not recall. The schism of distaste between our families, to hear my parents speak of bad blood and their associates gossip, has been a long-standing rivalry of politics and family history I never cared to understand. But this—what is the connection between my reclusive aunt and Madame Garcon that she provided the beautiful, bitter lemon cake for Aunt Melody's funeral? *How curious.*

Sterling deposits his burgundy umbrella beside another grouping of surprisingly similar umbrellas with intricate, bird-faced handles and mother-of-pearl eyes. *Definitely* curious.

Madame Garcon guides us through a charming entryway to a bright and airy parlor, where a table is neatly set with exquisite elements for tea.

Reclaimed and whitewashed wood floors match the fine tablecloth, while wide black and white stripes zigzag down the walls like zebra markings. Wrought iron accents weave through the space to hold it together, from the front door to the handrails trailing a narrow black path up the stairs. A cascade of blooming flowers adorns every available surface, each unique and each equally marvelous.

In the open floorplan, I count seven windows on five sides of the room, which seems impossible.

Clocks of all kinds cover the few spans of walls that aren't glass where the light shines through, and they mock my life, my art, and my heart of secrets and shadows.

But then Madame Garcon swings her full attention to me. If real life had stage lights for the heroine, this would be my singular moment in the spotlight. What I wouldn't give to go somewhere alone and touch up my makeup.

"What a lovely dress," the vivacious yet graceful woman says, taking in my outfit, which I must say, for this headline-catching moment, is suitably beautiful. It's a watercolor waterfall on canvas in dress form, very artistic. I feel my cheeks flush at her admiration, her compliment taking the edge off my nerves. "And who might you be?" she asks, and my anxiety returns with a tumult.

Sterling saves me. "Libby," he clears his throat lightly, hiding my identity, as we'd agreed, by using my childhood nickname, "is assisting me with our business today."

Not untrue, but also not fully true. Tricky use of words. Because today I'm Libby, his assistant with a classy laptop bag and eager to serve, not Elizabeth, the girl hiding behind the pen name she just inherited from her dead aunt, hoping for a future with her art.

If the lady of the manor senses my discomfort, she lets it go. "Lovely. How do you assist Sterling, Libby?"

"Oh," I begin awkwardly. I've been so busy worrying how she'll receive my pencil drawing, I haven't given a single thought to what my role of being assistant actually means.

Ticks from the multitude of clocks patter in the break of silence as Sterling gestures from behind the woman, our secret ear-tug-head-tilt indicating our business shall commence.

"She helps the art come alive with her very presence." He tucks his hand behind his red velvet waistcoat peppered with tiny ink-spot buttons. "As we discussed, Penelope, because you're restarting the auction, it will be the perfect occasion to debut Briar Rose's newest series, *Hearts*." The Madame nods. I'm assuming she doesn't know my aunt was Briar Rose—the most gifted pencil artist of her generation, and surely the most venerated in Loirehall's recent history. "Today we'll show you the inspiration, *The First Heart*. If you like it, you can auction the piece while you keep an originally commissioned portrait for your personal collection. Both will draw a crowd, and it will be splendid."

I freeze at Sterling's brazen grasping of an opportunity—my bald-headed and dapper benefactor-investor-wizardly-godfather never wastes one—and I should be grateful. It's my career, my art. I'd thought today's negotiation was just to claim a new portrait commission; clearly Sterling has other ideas, like adding *The First Heart* to the auction. He won't meet my gaze as he rambles on while cups sit empty before us—we haven't even had tea yet.

I fist the fabric of my dress but quickly let go lest anyone see my stress. Unveiling my first, heart wrenching drawing at a soirée filled with socialites and ghosts from my past is the very last thing I want to do. Ever.

Ever, ever, ever. Besides, my parents could very well show up at a society event like this, and that would be a nightmare.

Madame Garcon fluffs her frosted blue skirt—a color not unlike her eyes—into her white wooden chair with some difficulty because it's so poofy. "It has been so long since we've seen new art from Briar Rose, it's almost like she flew away."

I wonder at the look filling her face, eyes drawn inward for a moment, the iceberg with a world beneath the surface.

She continues, "Her talent precedes her, though she remains mysterious." To me, "And worry not, we'll have tea and treats shortly." She gestures for me to sit to her right.

My wing-backed chair feels like a throne, with curved armrests carved like streaming branches. I'm at the head of a glass table and I feel just about that fragile. Like everyone might see right through the depths of me, and liable to break at any moment.

Sterling launches into his spiel highlighting Briar Rose's art—her intuitive knack for capturing the heart of the collector through her bizarre yet beautiful portraits of doors, all in the timeless medium of charcoal. I already heard it earlier when he laid out our plan on our way through Upper Towne.

I school my expression so my face reflects none of the truth of my identity—I'm the assistant, *not* the artist. I busy myself, considering Sterling and my awe of how he somehow maneuvered events to capture *this* portrait commission from *this* family dynasty. This, my good fortune.

This. What an understated pronoun.

This place is wonderful. Impressions are powerful, as certain painters knew, and this home is magic from the moment one walks in. It's no small wonder that the highly photogenic setting and the gardens I'm glimpsing beyond the largest window will be the central feature for a sensational soirée. An event at which my work might be heavily featured, if this teaparty goes well.

I watch a second tick past on a clock with a black marble face and bronze first and second hands.

"What's the story behind all the clocks?" I wonder aloud, hiding the bitterness clawing for my tone.

I figure that's a pretty simple question, but sometimes the simplest of questions have complex answers, if they can be answered with any certainty at all. *Why can't you answer questions instead of asking them?* That's what my father used to say.

"The clocks." Madame Garcon smiles serenely, making a show of taking in the far wall, which is entirely covered from floor to ceiling with every imaginable version of a timepiece. Not a window in sight. "The clocks started as a joke that turned into my signature."

I decide I like her smile, but I wonder would she smile like that at me if she knew who I was. "So, it wasn't your idea?"

"Goodness, no!" she repeats, holding herself regally as if to tell us a timeless story. I wonder if she was the star of one, a long time ago. "The only person outside of time is God alone. If I *am* late, it's only because I am failing to overthrow the intrinsic property of the space we live in. Time isn't absolute. My perception of it just doesn't fit society's unfairly imposed restrictions. And since I am *not* God, I am mercilessly expected to adhere to arcane ideas of punctuality and timeliness." She ends her tirade with a sigh. "The only thing uniformly timely is tea."

Well, I did *not* expect that lecture on the nature of time and space. I wish for a sip of tea, but the teacups and I are waiting for our teapot companions and dainty sweets.

"I just have a thing for clocks, and my late husband had a unique sense of humor," she concludes and Sterling smiles that Cheshire smile, like he's party to a story I couldn't even imagine.

But thankfully, Sterling brings our conversation back around to the present.

They descend into a serious tête-à-tête regarding the upcoming event, and I zone out when they start talking about long tables, because I'm not sure if they're metaphorical or not. All this normal talk has made me a bit queasy, if only because it's wholly unexpected: this welcoming, familiar feeling permeating the house and mannerisms of the sworn enemy of my family—or so I've always been told. The reality, sitting here as a young woman almost finally of age, feels quite different.

My nauseated feeling perfectly matches the near-despair I feel when my efforts to readjust the off-center linen napkin in front of me make it much, much worse.

I swirl my fingertips beneath the table, secretly drawing on the seat of the chair beside my crossed legs. My stomach twists in the predictable way it does whenever I venture into the world, encountering everyday terrors of misaligned corners and mismatched knick-knacks. There are even four different sized jars for the same gorgeous tiger lilies scattered around on piles of books on random side tables, all their stems cut to different heights.

They might be beautiful, but all I want to do is take them away somewhere less cluttered. Off the counter and away from the possibility they might get knocked over. Somewhere safe, where they belong. My drawing fingers pause as I take a break from pondering the room and suck in a deep breath to calm the quaking inside.

It's all equally distracting. Equally fascinating. Equally terrifying.

This is my problem. *Does anyone else see the world differently and feel like an outsider to anything bright and beautiful?* I quench my secrets and secret behaviors, stifling my impulses until I'm alone, before they turn me into an outcast, where people speak over me as if I'm a piece of furniture or heaven forbid, art, there to be seen and not heard.

How I wish there were things I had neither seen nor heard.

I shake my head out from childhood memories, glancing away from the window-wall to clock-wall, my eyes return to the enormous grandfather clock that caught my eye earlier. Familiar insecurity flares in the too-familiar neighborhood with the too-familiar grandfather clock—and of course, the Old Woods not far off.

It reminds me of when I found myself in a sterile and falsely welcoming office after the events of that fateful birthday, long-ago. They had an oversized clock in the waiting room, and it always scared me when the top of the hour came because a frightful cacophony of noise signaled the start of when strangers with long acronyms after their names asked me questions that made no sense.

Why can't you answer questions instead of asking them?

With my father's voice in my head, my seven-year-old-self answered in kind.

Why did you wander alone in the woods? *Is wondering the same as wandering?*

Why haven't your parents ever seen your friend? *Do you think he's still searching without me?*

Why don't you play this game with other children? *Would anyone else want to?*

Why did you hide by that tree? *Do you think I hid something?*

Did you find what you were looking for? *Have you?*

They wondered what I wanted to *do* when I grew up. They never asked who I wanted to *be*.

Seven years ago

The moon watched, pale as my inner misery that only lightened during those stolen rooftop moments. My mind filled with ceaseless thoughts, my soul pining with endless longing. If only my longing could pull me out and up by my arms—like the dying rays of sun, like the first appearing light of morning.

"You don't sleep at night like a normal person."

"You join me," I accused, thankful for the way he'd found me, years ago.

I'd been terrified the first time he spoke to me out of the dark that fateful night—me, a frightened girl afraid to sleep after the seventh-birthday fiasco when I ran away from my own birthday party and broke my hand from a fall in the forest.

The broken heart hurt worse.

When they finally found me, an ambulance didn't just arrive to take me to the hospital. There was another for Grandmother, who'd also fallen—a heart attack, or was it a stroke?—but when I left the hospital to come home, she did not.

Later that day, news arrived of a car accident, which left my friend a lost orphan boy.

My birthday was a tragedy.

Because of my injury, my parents—distracted by Grandmother's shocking death and having long given up on getting me to talk or eat or sleep—thought I would stay put. I spent the rest of that awful afternoon on the roof, but that only got me sunburnt. So then, at sunset, I worked up the courage to return to the Old Woods, alone.

But I wasn't alone. There was a villain, a shadow, and my bravery was rewarded with more pain—how was I to know what cursed thing I'd find in the woods? How was I to carry the burden of accidental knowledge at what I'd seen buried in that forest? How was I to know that the tragic events that concluded my really-bad seventh birthday would be confirmed as sinister if I returned to the Old Woods?

I told no one. And that's when the nightmares started.

Awakening near midnight, screaming, sweating, shivering, seven-year-old me awkwardly had crawled through the dormer window onto the roof. Aching, broken hand, my skin on fire, and heartsick, I vowed never to return to the memories of the forest, hoping to be alone to end my cursed birthday, but glad I wasn't.

Because that's when I found him, the boy who hid in shadows kept me company during the worst day of my year, on the worse day of his life. He was there that first midnight, at the end of that really-bad-seventh-birthday, and since then, he showed up without fail, every birthday. Suspicion grew into mockery and blossomed into an annual companionship of adolescent angst watered with shared boxes of cookies, years of summer midnights on my birthday shared across separate roofs with this strange, reclusive boy.

Here, on our sixth summer together, while I knew he was four-
teen, to twelve-year-old me, he'd never quite grown up. I knew he
knew who I was—that I was his childhood friend from the forest.
We just never spoke of it. So maybe he and I had grown up too
much, for we'd never returned to play in the forest or speak of
happy days before both our worlds turned upside down.

"I'm just bored." Typical teenager, his voice kept breaking and
he cleared his throat to cover it up.

"Whatever." My maturity was not a hallmark of our interaction
either, philosophical interludes aside.

"What would you do if you weren't out here?"

"Lie in bed and cry," I replied instantly. It was easy to tell the
truth, speaking it from the rooftop in the comforting darkness of
anonymity where we preserved this freedom without expectations,
hiding our faces.

I used to be the kind of girl who faced her fears. After that fateful
birthday, I'd been hiding, having learned my lesson about freedom
and finding answers.

"Why can't you sleep?" He'd never asked before, not in all the
summers before this one.

I wasn't sure if I could answer. "I don't know, maybe the
light keeps me awake." That wasn't it—because it was dark at
night—but I'd flown through excuses with abandon over the years,
lost without a heading and suffering without meaning.

"My aunt has a saying about that."

"What?" I asked. "Faith, trust, and pixie dust?"

"She says there won't be any light in heaven because love itself
will be light enough."

"How does that make any sense?"

"I don't know," his shadow seemed to shrug. "Maybe we'll be weightless there and just float around. I don't take anything she says seriously."

I tilted my head at a particularly bright star above, not believing the tone he'd put on. His aunt made an impression on him and often came up in our conversations. "How will that help me sleep?"

"Maybe it'll be dark."

I shivered. "I don't want to live forever in the dark."

"You know what I've always wanted to do?" he asked me and the night sky.

I never could keep up with his nonsensical change of topics. Hitting the absolute ceiling of sense was easier under the stars and always made me dizzy.

"What?" I decided to delay his moment and drag down his wings before liftoff. He'd tell me regardless, and I'd grown used to the wild feeling of trying to keep up to his random trains of thought. "Memorize a whole book and find the world in it underground?" I guessed. "Travel to every country you can't spell and after that search the stars for untamed places you could name? Fight a dragon?"

He shuffled closer and flicked my toes. "In your dreams."

"I don't dream." I fingered the slats on the roof, avoiding brownish slivers and finding a loose piece to wiggle free. I held it in my palm for a moment before tossing it to the ground, where it landed with a tiny clatter.

"Liar." He was always very good at verbalizing the lies in my life—if he could name his own, or share them with me, maybe he'd be less mad.

"Well then, what?" To my right, the bright star caught my eye again. Persistent little hopeful thing. "What have you always wanted to do?"

"Fly."

"What? A plane? You've never been on a plane?"

"No, I've been on a plane," he grunted, with adequate levels of boredom and offense in his tone. "I mean fly, like, myself. Up in the air, right now."

"That's impossible." I snorted at unreachable stars, but lifted my arms so the linen blew in the breeze.

"I brought you these." His shadow hands shook something across the short expanse between the shed and the second story roof.

"Why?" My newly twelve-year-old self really was the opposite of charitable. But I extended my hand and he dropped a tiny stick onto my waiting palm. "What—"

"Sparklers. I was going to light them, you know, since it's your birthday."

And the anniversary of your parents death. I hadn't forgotten. I cherished that this shadow boy ended each of my terrible-awful-bad birthday days with brooding, snarky, reliable companionship on our opposite roofs. I didn't know for sure where he lived, because I'd only seen him at midnight these past birthday-nights under the stars, twice even when it rained. Part of me was glad we never saw each other in real life, in the light of day. For he was my old friend, and I didn't know how to tell him what I'd seen in the Old Woods, or if he'd forgive me if he knew.

Instead I whispered, "You didn't forget." *You never forget.*

Ignoring the gratefulness in my tone for every birthday he'd kept me company, he asked brusquely, "Are you too afraid, or are we going to do this?"

"I'm not afraid." The trampoline below, tucked in the corner of my backyard beneath the eaves of the shed of the townhouse beside mine, loomed larger than life in the inky blackness.

I couldn't imagine falling so far, especially on purpose.

He lit a flame, framed in shadow. Teenage boys always have lighters on them, apparently. "These are the stars. Even falling can be flying if you soar through the lights."

"Who's philosophical now?"

One, then two, sparklers started sparking. Then he lit mine. I never saw his face but for the shifting shadows dancing in the dark. He reminded me of a sparkler. I was never quite sure when the light began, but the unexpected bright in my darkness fizzled out unexpectedly after every midnight when he left.

"You first." He tossed them onto the trampoline as if they were a meteor shower. "It's perfectly safe."

"What if I fall?" I couldn't think. My hand fisted around my own sparking sparkler.

"You won't fall."

Precious few moments remained. "How can you be sure?" I threw my sparkler like a shooting star.

"Because you can fly."

Then I followed the light and jumped.

Acknowledgments

Dear reader,

Thank you, so much, for reading. If you're willing to continue a little bit more, I would love to tell you about the many wonderful people who have helped me along this journey. I pray I don't forget anyone (if I do, know I love you, and I'll make it up in Hearts!). So, here are the stars:

Thank you, AJ Skelly, for being an extraordinary CEO, fellow tea-drinker, and lover of books. Your enthusiasm, authorpreneurial spirit, and energy are inspiring. And most of all, thank you for believing in my fairytales and the vision of Heartbooks. You have been a personal and professional support and I appreciate every one of the thousands of texts you always reply to, and all the openness you have for letting me learn this publishing industry. Here's to more fun, more t-shirts and mugs, and many more books!

Beta readers are my superpower. That's right. Any cool supposed powers I have (I don't, but let's pretend) should all be credited to other people, and they are just the best. There are so many readers who saw this story in the earlier stages. You know who you are, and if I haven't already, I'll be chasing you to beta read the next one, if you want. Thank you all.

My critique group through Realm Makers is the absolute best. These wonderful ladies see potential, they're a safe place to share new writing and experiment with wild ideas, they pray, they encourage, they like my silly comments in Google Docs and they are the best. Thank you Kaitlyn, Andi, Kayla, and Kara! And Kaitlyn! You were along for the ride with this story as it happened. Would that everyone had a friend to tell about their super-secret work in progress. You were the first person to hear about Nicholas and Penelope's story, and the first to hear any of my writing news. You've been with me through every rejection and graciously joined me through those snow-filled, K-Drama loving moments. Thank you! It's worth it!

Also and especially, thank you Brigitte! You have combed through the spaces between lines in my manuscripts to find hidden gems, but you're even more priceless! What else can I say but thank you, and also, please please please read my next story and help me. I hope every author is lucky enough to find a reader + friend like you, because sometimes, our friends see the story we're trying to write before we do, and that is a wonderful thing.

Thank you to my editors: Jessica and Sarah. The idea of my words in ink on a page is exciting instead of scary because of the confidence I gained through your insightful, detailed, and thoughtful edits.

Thank you to my agent, Rachel McMillan, for your wisdom and belief in my writing.

My family has cheered on my writing, so much so, we had to make publishing this book a family affair. It means the world that you let me share your art! Adam—Thank you for my chapter headings! I think your "snowflake necklace crown of metal flowers" turned out alright. (That's real text from our Whatsapp conversation, seriously.) Mom—your creativity and belief in Heartbooks (thirteen years ago or so we first talked about Heartbooks) have been around as long as I've had the idea, thank you. (The pretty lettering and the adorable map were all her!) Dad—you never let me give up on the writing, thank you.

Thank you to my kids for reminding me of the real world: to my boys for showing me what chivalry and strength are, and to my little princess who is bold and brave in a way I want to be someday.

To my husband, without whom I never would have been able to write or do all these author things.

And to Jesus, without you, what reason would I have to write? Thank you.

My hands waver above the
aged typewriter. Letters call
to me to find their meaning.
I can't imagine what brought
me here, to him.
Fate, destiny, all my

I've never been able to
find the one story that
mattered to me.
Until now.

THE AUTHOR

Brittany's fascination with Wonderland may have given her the courage to exclusively use a sparkly Cinderella book bag while completing her First Class Honours degree in Greek & Roman Civilization and Political Science at the National University of Ireland, Maynooth. She's travelled to over twenty-five countries and has walked the Great Wall of China in Beijing, the Acropolis in Athens, Table Mountain in Cape Town, and Ipanema in Rio. She also once lived in a Circus.

You can find Brittany drinking tea, reading, and chasing her three kids, usually at the same time. If that fails, you'll find her writing starcrossed romance with timeless endings or on Instagram @brittanyedenauthor oversharing pictures of the scenery around her and her husband's home in Vancouver, Canada, and commenting passionately about C.S. Lewis, K-Dramas, Wonder Woman, Bournville chocolate, and Irish tea.

Find out more about her stories at brittanyeden.com and by subscribing to her newsletter *From Eden To Eternity*.

QUILL & FLAME

Quill & Flame
PUBLISHING HOUSE

Find other Quill & Flame titles at www.quillandflame.com or @quill.and.flame.publishers on Instagram.

Stay tuned for more short stories as well as future releases from Quill & Flame Publishing House.

Join Quill & Flame Book Tours by emailing quillandflamepub lishinghouse@gmail.com.

Find other Quill & Titles releasing soon!

Making Magik: A Magik Prep Academy Anthology 2023

Fortified by V. Romas Burton February 2023
Of Flame & Frost by AJ Skelly March 2023
By Light & Love by Anna Augustine April 2023
R.E.M. by Ashley Schaller May 2023
Hearts by Brittany Eden June 2023
Heart of the Sea by Moriah Chavis August 2023
By Blade & Blood by Anna Augustine September 2023
Shadowcast by Crystal D. Grant October 2023
Magic & Mistletoe: A Quill & Flame Christmas Anthology
December 2023

How many

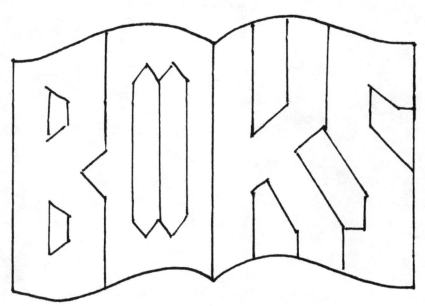

have you filled?